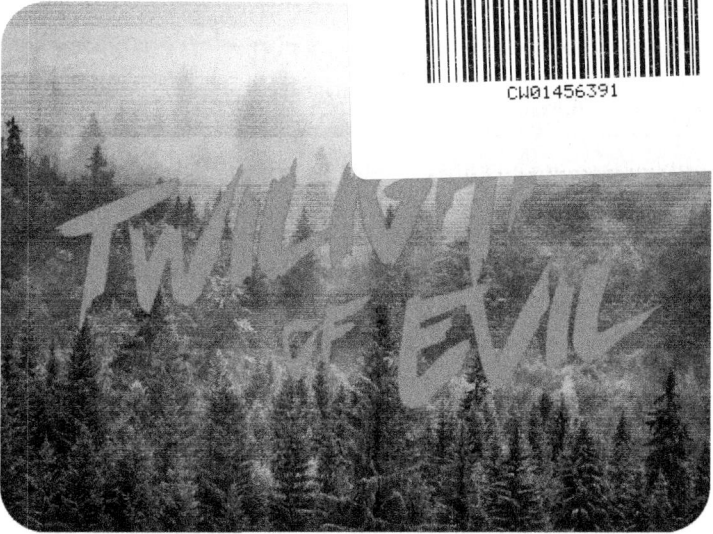

Twilight of Evil
By P. J. Thorndyke

2024 by Copyright © P. J. Thorndyke

CHAPTER 1

Northern California, 1987.

Mount Lenzi was a black hump against the deep blue of the clear night sky, the full moon dusting the tips of the pines and redwoods with silver. Deep within the gloom of the trees, the beams of four flashlights cut through the darkness as a shadowy congregation made its way to the peak.

"Wait up, you guys," said Todd Cates, the heavier of the four. "I'm about to have a fucking heart attack here."

Red-faced at the best of times, sweat ran down from the shaved sides of Todd's blond mullet, glistening in the moonlight and soaking the neckline of his gray Metallica t-shirt.

"I told you we should have driven the van all the way up," said Gary Winters, a gangly kid whose arms were a little too long for his baseball tee, as he turned around and aimed his flashlight into Todd's face. "But you didn't think it could make it."

"She could make it, I just don't wanna get her all scratched up. You saw how close those trees were back there, now get that fucking light outta my face!"

"We're almost there, Todd," said Brooke McKenna; Todd's girlfriend; a snub-nosed girl with blonde, frizzy hair held in a side ponytail by a pink scrunchie.

"Thank Christ," Todd gasped. "Remind me why we had to haul our asses all the way up here to do the ritual instead of in my basement where there's, y'know, a couch and beer."

"For the right aura," said the fourth member of the group; Toby Johnson, a sullen kid who looked like every parent's worst nightmare. He had shaggy hair dyed black, eyeliner and a black Venom t-shirt emblazoned with the sigil of Baphomet.

"Right, right," Todd grumbled. "The fucking *aura*. We don't know if this is just a crock of shit."

"It might be," said Toby. "But just in case, let's try and do it right."

They reached the bald peak of the mountain and surveyed the view. Deep redwood forest carpeted the hills for as far as the eye could see. The only signs of humanity were the headlights of vehicles on the highway far below and the distant cluster of lights that was the town of Crimson Bay.

Brooke pulled up the collar of her denim jacket and hugged her arms. Summer was over but the dark purpose of their trip up the mountain that night would have sent a chill down her spine no matter the weather. "This won't take long, right, Toby?"

"As long as it takes to burn a few things and say a few words," Toby replied.

"Good," said Todd as he recovered his breath and looked around at the trees that seemed to whisper in the wind. "I don't wanna spend any more time up here than we have to."

"Scared, Todd?" asked Gary with a grin.

Todd extended his middle finger. "Eat dick, twerp."

Mount Lenzi had been the site of a massacre five years earlier when a ninth grader camping trip had been cut short by the escape of Anthony Stevens, a local child molester who had been sent to prison back in 1968. Forever remembered as the night *He* came home, Stevens had butchered a few people in town, stolen a jeep and followed the school trip up the mountain. Then, under cover of darkness, he had killed one ninth grader, a teacher and three of the four seniors who were helping out on the trip, taking revenge on the town that had sent him to prison. The cops managed to close in on him later that night and Sheriff Weiss had put three bullets in Stevens's back as he had fled into the woods.

But his body had never been found.

That last part was the source of many local legends and slumber party spook stories. Anytime somebody went missing, it was Anthony Stevens who had taken them. Any noise in the backyard at night was Anthony Stevens, come to claim another victim. But, with the passing of five years, nobody seriously believed that the infamous mass-murderer was still wandering around the woods surrounding Crimson Bay. He had died that night, and his body was rotting somewhere in those woods. Nevertheless, his legend lived on.

"Everybody got their totems?" Toby asked.

"Yeah," said Brooke, pulling a small teddy bear keychain from her jacket pocket. It was only a cheap thing from a rack in a mom-and-pop store, but she held it gently, as if frightened of something happening to it. It had been her sister's and she had taken it from the frozen mausoleum of her room without her parents noticing.

"Right here," said Gary, holding out a tin whistle of the kind gym coaches use. It had a red string attached.

"What's yours?" Brooke asked Toby.

Toby rummaged in the pocket of his ripped jeans and pulled out a white plastic bottle opener with 'Coors' written on it.

"A bottle opener?" Brooke asked him.

"Yeah," said Toby. "It's been in the kitchen drawer since before I was born. Dad always used it when he came home from work."

"I kind of feel left out here," said Todd with a dopey grin. "I'm the only one who didn't bring something to the party."

"Don't even joke about it, dipshit," said Brooke. "You're lucky you don't have anything to contribute."

"All right, all right," said Todd, holding his hands up. "Just trying to lighten the mood. Jeez."

Fooling around with the occult on a haunted mountaintop at the dead of night with a full moon shining down might have been nothing but fun and games for any other group of teens, but it was given a somber sense of purpose by the personal investment these kids had. All of them, with the exception of Todd, had lost somebody to Anthony Stevens's bloody knife that night five years ago. Brooke, her big sister. Toby, his dad. Gary, his mom. All of their lives had been ruined by forces beyond their control. And there wasn't anything they wouldn't do to turn the clock back.

The germ of the idea had been incubated during a beer and weed session in Todd's basement two weeks before. Todd's folks were often away, and he pretty much had the place to himself. His family basement was the perfect hideout for high school wasters who just wanted to get high and not think about the world. The summer holidays were winding down and school started next week. The gloom of September hung over the four of them like a lengthy prison sentence.

Of all of them, only Gary had gotten out of Crimson Bay that summer. His dad had a new girlfriend, some academic loser who lived down in Big Sur. Gary didn't know what his dad saw in her. She lived in a goddamn camper for one thing and when she wasn't slumming it like white trash, she was in Europe or the Middle East scrabbling about in the dirt for bits of old crap nobody cared about.

Suzanne was an archaeologist, and, being a geography teacher, his dad thought that was a real turn on. Hell, he probably saw her as an upgrade to his deceased wife who had only been the school coach and not particularly book smart. Gary could summon nothing but resentment for the woman his dad was trying to pass off as his stepmom and loathed being dragged down to Big Sur to stay with her in her pokey little camper where, even in his bunk up front, he could feel the goddamn bed in the back shaking at night.

The camper was full of old junk too. Academic books, bits of pottery with labels attached to them like it was some sort of half-assed museum on wheels. Suzanne's latest kick was medieval churches in France which, to Gary's mind, sounded like she was *trying* to be boring. What the hell could you find in an old church?

Well, as it turned out, she had found something that at least piqued some mild curiosity in her surly stepson. He had pilfered it and brought it round to Todd's basement to show his friends.

"She found a Latin translation of some old grimoire," he told them. "It's only a fragment of the original tome. It was found beneath the altar of a deconsecrated church in France where a heretical priest once held sway."

"Gnarly," said Toby, lounging on the shag carpet, a joint hanging from his lips. "Was he like a satanist or something?"

"I don't know, I just heard what my dad's girlfriend said while they were on the wine one night." He pulled a dogeared school notebook from his back pocket and riffled through it. "Suzanne translated it into English. I doubt she'll notice it's gone, there's enough bits of paper and notebooks to sink a ship in her camper. Look here, there's all sorts of sick stuff like rituals and prophecies, a guide to demons, resurrection ..."

"Hold up," Brooke said, lifting her head up from where she was resting it on Todd's ample chest. "Resurrection?"

"That's what it says."

"As in, bringing people back from the dead?"

"Yeah, that's pretty much what 'resurrection' means," Gary said sarcastically.

"What does it say?"

"You want me to read it?"

"Yeah."

Gary cleared his throat.

"Wait a minute," said Toby. "This place doesn't exactly give off the right aura for dealing with the occult."

"Aura?" Todd asked. "What are you getting at, Johnson?"

Toby looked around at the wood paneling and rusty metal shelves piled with junk. "No offence, dude, but your basement isn't exactly the right place to summon the dead or anything."

"Unless you're summoning dead roaches and rats," said Gary.

"Screw you guys," said Todd. "I let you hang out here and you talk shit about my folks' house?"

"Just messing with you, man," said Gary. "But maybe Toby has a point. We should totally try out some of these rituals. But only if we do it properly with, like, candles and daggers and stuff. Toby, you know how all that shit works, right? You've done a black mass before?"

"Well, uh, yeah but that's like, psychodrama and stuff. Satan is just a figurehead for man's primal instincts. He doesn't really exist, at least not as an actual entity."

"Gimme that notebook," said Brooke, thrusting her hand out at Gary. He handed it over and she leafed through it. "From the *Liber Ivonis*, tenth to eleventh century," she said, reading the heading of Gary's stepmom's translation. She thumbed through it, looking for the resurrection ritual. "What are all these long black lines?"

"I guess Suzanne wasn't able to translate those bits," said Gary. "Or maybe they were missing in the original manuscript. She said it was pretty beat up like it had been in a fire or something."

"There's some stuff here in another language that she wasn't able to translate," Brooke continued. "There's a sidenote penciled in; 'Sumerian? – ask Professor Campbell.'" She looked up from the notebook, her eyes deep in thought. "Imagine if we could use this to bring back the people who were taken from us. The ones that bastard Anthony Stevens stole from us."

"Wouldn't they be all like ... *zombies*?" Todd said. "It was five years ago. They'd all be rotten flesh and bones and stuff by now."

The other three glared at him. "Not my mom," said Gary. "She was cremated."

"Yeah, well ..." said Todd, running his fingers through his hair. "It wouldn't work in her case, anyway, right?"

"Yes, it would," said Brooke, still engrossed in the ritual. "It says here that the sprits of the dead can be manifested in corporeal form, even if the ... uh, *raw material* – gross – is no longer existent."

"You don't think all this bullshit is the real deal, do you, babe?" said Todd.

Brooke shrugged. "I don't know. But what do you say we give it a try and see what happens?"

"A big fat nothing, that's what. Some medieval dude wrote down a bunch of crap about resurrection, doesn't mean we have to take it seriously."

"What have we got to lose?"

"Nothing. Sure, I'm in. But if you dickwads think my basement isn't grand enough for occult rituals, then where are we gonna do it?"

"Toby?" Gary asked. "You're the occult expert."

"The top of Mount Lenzi," Toby said. "It's a landmark and it's where Brooke's sister and Gary's mom were killed. It's bound to have some real energy and the peak will be a good conduit."

"Jesus ..." said Todd with a disbelieving grin. "All your talk about energies and shit. I thought God was dead and Satan wasn't real. Now you're sounding like you believe this crap will actually work."

Toby shrugged his shoulders. "Worth a shot."

And that was how it started. Four high-school kids, each of them troubled in their own way, keen to do something, *try* something. For kicks. To alleviate boredom. To feel like they were taking back control of their destroyed lives in some way.

With Gary's permission, Toby had taken the notebook home with him and studied it along with various other cheap occult paperbacks he had in his possession including *The Satanic Bible* and a tome on Enochian magic. The notebook Gary had stolen wasn't exactly heavy on how to do the actual ritual. It provided the words to say but all the stuff about burning totems under a full moon were all Toby's insertions.

Now that the four of them were standing atop Mount Lenzi beneath the silver disk of the moon with the cool wind sighing all around them, it didn't seem like quite so much fun. Further along, as the peak reached its highest point, the charred remains of a fire lookout cabin stood against the sky like the blackened bones of some long dead creature. One of the last in the state, it had been disused for a couple of years before local kids had burned it down. Broken beer and wine cooler bottles littered the area. The four occultists weren't the only ones who partied at the top of the mountain.

They watched as Toby made a small campfire in the shadow of the ruined lookout cabin, dousing a clump of tinder he had brought from home with lighter fluid. As the flames grew and Toby fed it with dry sticks, they all began to appreciate its warm glow, but the grim purpose of the fire still hung over them like a cold shadow.

"All right," said Toby. "I'm going to read the ritual and when I indicate, each of you place your totem on the flames."

They all nodded, and Toby began. "Hail your Satanic Majesty! Hail Mighty Master of Evil! Most respected foe of Jehovah and all his angels! Hear me, your loyal and devoted servant! Grant my request to bring the dead back from beyond the veil between worlds!"

At a nod from Toby, they placed their totems on the burning pile of twigs. The setting, the mood and Toby's satanic words made an almost comical contrast to the pure innocence of the teddy keychain, gym whistle and Coors bottle opener but, as the flames licked at them and started to consume them, their innocence melted away and they became ugly, twisted things. The pink fur of the teddy blackened as it burned away, leaving only its wide and staring, glassy eyes. The tin whistle grew tarnished, its red cord burned away, and the plastic bottle opener melted and bubbled, turning from white to a sickly brown.

As they watched the destruction of these items that had belonged to their loved ones, Toby read the untranslated portion of the text, taking his time with the unusual words, pronouncing them as best he could.

"Artát, nibórtsima atrázah. Rrítnat, vonam nozísnam raboznázah. Adnumus aspor, sihrad rukiah azdóredsnud. Adnak, adnak, adnak."

It may have been their imaginations, but each of them swore later that they felt the wind pick up as he spoke the words. The tops of the trees bent and shook, the breeze sounding like whispers as it passed between them.

"Hear me, Satan, Lord of the Dead!" Toby continued. "Bring back that which sleeps in stone and clay! Hear me, you doorkeeper who guards your portals, who swallows souls and who gulps down the corpses of the dead who pass you by when they are allotted to the House of Destruction. May you guide the dead, may you open the portals, may the earth open its caverns! Hear me, lost soul in the Kingdom of the Dead, take your head, collect your bones, gather your limbs, shake the earth from your flesh! The hidden ones worship you, the great ones surround you, the watchers wait on you. Arise! Arise! Arise!"

There was silence but for the wind in the treetops and the sputtering and crackling of the offerings in the fire, nearly wholly consumed now. A single eye from Brooke's disintegrated teddy keychain bubbled and hissed before it dripped down into the glowing embers.

Predictably, it was Todd who broke the uneasy silence. "So ... now what?"

"Now, we wait," said Toby.

"What, up here?" said Todd. "For how long?"

"No, not up here. We don't know where or when the dead will return but I think it's safe to say they won't materialize before us on this mountaintop."

"What do we do then?" asked Gary. "I thought you had all this occult stuff figured out?"

"I just read the words and chose the place and time," Toby snapped irritably.

"I still think it's a crock of shit," said Todd.

"Why don't we just go home?" asked Brooke. "Nothing else is gonna happen up here tonight and I don't want to stand around in the woods all night. If the spell worked, then I guess we'll know about it soon enough."

"Yeah, I'm with Brooke," said Gary. "We've done what we came to do."

"Jesus, talk about an anticlimax," said Todd as they stamped out the fire and headed back down the mountain.

"What did you expect?" asked Toby. "*Night of the Living Dead*?"

"I didn't expect shit and that's what we got!"

Their voices receded as they disappeared down the trail to where Todd's Dodge Tradesman was parked. The wind continued to blow in their absence, passing between the darkened trees like a voice from beyond. It rolled down the slopes of Mount Lenzi, carrying its message through the woods and down to the gushing river. By the time it reached the highway it had dissipated.

But something in those woods had heard its message and had awakened.

CHAPTER 2

The picnic ground was a recent addition to the mountain trail and was little more than a small patch of dirt on the shoulder of Mount Lenzi overlooking the river. It had been cleared of trees and a couple of benches had been dropped there where hikers and families spent sunny afternoons. It was late at night and only one vehicle was parked there now; a beige motorhome which, despite its size, bounced up and down on its suspension courtesy of the activity within.

"Oh, God!" Patrick gasped as he hoisted Teresa up and down with his hips, her naked thighs straddling his middle.

She arched her back, her long, dark ponytail swaying from side to side, her face screwed up in ecstasy as he thrust harder and deeper. He reached up a hand, and grabbed her left breast, squeezing it and thumbing the nipple. Jesus, she was beautiful!

Sweat stood out on her bronzed skin which was dappled by the moonlight shining in through the gap in the drapes. The air was thick and clammy with their mingled breath and their bodies felt like they were on fire.

"Don't stop!" Teresa gasped.

Christ, he didn't think he could hold on! He tried, for her sake, to keep himself from erupting early but knew it was a losing battle.

She raked her nails down his chest and squeezed his cock even harder with her abdominal muscles. That was it. That was all he could take.

"Oh, come on!" Teresa whined as he shot his load into his rubber Johnny and writhed beneath her. "I wasn't there yet!"

"I'm ... sorry, baby!" he gasped.

She sighed and got off him, clambering off the bed and turning to enter the small bathroom compartment. As she left, he watched her perfect ass move in the pale moonlight and knew he was the luckiest guy in the whole world.

"Gimmie a few minutes and we can go again," he croaked.

"I might be *asleep* in a few minutes, Patrick," Teresa said as she switched on the small light above the sink.

Patrick lay back and squeezed his eyes shut in frustration. If he didn't up his game and soon, he could risk losing Teresa. To be honest, he was surprised he had bagged her in the first place. The statuesque brunette had made quite a splash on her first day in the company's accounting department, turning heads and causing many sly looks and winks among the men. Their collective jaws had just about hit the floor when she had started dating Patrick. He suspected his motorhome played some part in it. All along, he'd done his best to insinuate that he was loaded but the truth was, it was his dad's motorhome and if she found *that* out, then it would definitely be over.

Other guys were waiting like that slick Ed Jones bastard in marketing. He'd expressed a concrete interest in Teresa, and he had a Ferrari for Christ's sake. He'd heard him joking in the office on Friday about how he'd like to bang her, knowing full well that Patrick was within ear shot. The other guys had yukked it up while Patrick had sat there, crimson-faced, knowing that a challenge had been issued that dated back to when their common ancestor had fallen out of his tree. It was ape against ape and Patrick entirely lacked the conviction of an alpha male.

Teresa gave out a sudden screech of terror and came hurtling out of the bathroom compartment, flinging herself at Patrick.

"What is it?" he cried as she scrambled beneath the bedsheets.

"There's somebody out there!" she wailed. "Somebody looked in the bathroom window at me!"

A cold chill grasped Patrick's heart. He had thought they were miles away from anybody. They hadn't seen any other vehicles on the trail that evening and had assumed they had the picnic area to themselves. "It's probably just kids," he said, trying to calm his own nerves as much as Teresa's. "Was it a kid's face?"

"I don't know, it was all in shadow!"

"Maybe it was just the shadow of one of the trees ..."

She glared at him. "I did not jump at a goddamn *shadow*, Patrick, I saw *somebody* out there!"

"Maybe they're lost and wondered if somebody was home," he said. "They'll probably just move on. He put his arm protectively around her shoulders and reached in to cup her breast. "Let's just lie here and ..."

"Are you kidding?" Teresa yelled, grabbing his hand and thrusting it away from her. "We are not getting down to it when some creep is wandering around outside trying to get a peek in at us! Get out there and tell them to get lost!"

"M ... me?"

"Well, I sure as hell am not going out there!"

Well, that was it. It was alpha male time. He had to go out there or any chance of banging Teresa in the future went down the crapper. He pictured Ed Jones's shit-eating grin and the guffawing faces of all the other men in the office.

He got up, pulled the condom off his suddenly flaccid dick with a wet snap and tossed it in the trash before putting on his bathrobe and belting it around the middle. He wished he had some sort of weapon – a gun or a bat or something – but there wasn't anything like that in the RV.

He went into the dinette and opened a drawer. Teresa watched from the sleeping compartment, the bedsheets pulled up to her chin, as he selected a kitchen knife.

It's just kids, he told himself as he slipped on his shoes and opened the side door. *Only kids*. He'd make a big show of giving them hell and hope to God they weren't psycho punks on drugs and then dive back into the grateful arms of Teresa who would tell him what a man he was.

He stepped down onto the dirt and looked at the silent trees that surrounded the picnic area in a semicircle. At his back, he heard the rushing of the river.

"Hello?" he called, cursing the reedy sound of his voice. That wasn't going to impress anybody, including Teresa. He cleared his throat and tried again, aiming deeper his time. "Who's out there? If any fucker out there wants to tangle with, me, just know that I'm armed with seven inches of cold steel!"

No answer but the gently sighing trees. Anybody might be hiding in those shadows.

Feeling slightly pleased with his tough guy act, he crept around the side of the RV to make sure no joker was loitering behind it. Nobody was there. He turned and made his way back. As he rounded the rear of the motorhome, he slammed straight into a man's chest, his heart rising into his throat, choking off his cry of alarm.

The man was tall but not particularly heavyset. In fact, there was something horribly thin about him and the stench he gave off was goddamned unholy. Patrick looked up into the stranger's face and the knife tumbled from his hand and clattered to the dirt as he found himself paralyzed with fear.

"Wh ... Wha ..." he managed before the stranger's hands locked around his neck, bony thumbs digging in deep, strangling him with a strength that defied the wiry frame beneath stinking, ragged clothes.

Patrick gasped and wheezed, grabbing his attacker's forearms and trying desperately to loosen the vice-like grip that was cutting off his air supply. It was no good. This man – this *creature* – whatever he was, was simply too strong. He found himself being forced to his knees which buckled beneath him.

The stranger released him but, before Patrick could contemplate the notion that he might be spared, the man seized the kitchen knife from the ground and brought it tip-down in a whirling arc, embedding it in the side of Patrick's neck.

Inside the motorhome, Teresa screamed as Patrick's body was slammed against the window, cracking the glass. As he slid to one side, a bloody smear was left in his wake. She screamed again when she saw his killer through the reddened glass. It was the same shadowed face that had peered in at her when she had been in the bathroom and now it had killed Patrick and was coming for her.

She ducked down as the shadow moved around to the other side of the motorhome, passing the window on its way to the door. In her terror-wracked mind, Teresa knew she would die if she let him in and she made a mad dash to the dinette, seizing the door handle just as it started to turn.

"Go away, you fucking psycho!" she yelled as she hauled on the doorhandle with all her might.

The man on the other side was too strong and, the handle dug cruelly into her palm as it was forced down.

Inch by inch, the door opened until the gap was wide enough for the kitchen knife to slide down its length, cutting Teresa's forearm.

She cried out and fell on her ass, blood streaming from a long, red line along her arm. The door to the motorhome was flung wide and the silhouette of the man filled the doorframe, black against the moonlight.

Teresa scrabbled backwards as she tried to retreat into the sleeping compartment, her palms and heels slipping in her own blood, slick on the linoleum floor. The figure clambered into the motorhome and Teresa bawled in terror, getting to her feet and launching herself into the sleeping compartment, slamming the flimsy wood-paneled door behind her.

She fumbled with the lock just as the weight of the killer slammed against the door. Teresa pushed herself against it, her feet digging into the shag carpet. The knife blade punctured the wood, seven inches of razor-sharp stainless steel emerging mere inches from Teresa's face, sending splinters across the room.

As the killer jerked the knife free, Teresa had no choice but to fall back or risk being impaled by the next thrust. She scrambled up onto the bed and pulled the sheets up around her in helpless terror as the knife burst through the door in a second spot. After wrenching it free, the killer began hurling his weight at the door again and again. On the third try, the lock broke and the door slammed back on its hinges.

Teresa grabbed the lamp from the nightstand and ripped its cord free from the plug socket. The killer stomped into the compartment, knife raised in an overarm grip. She swung the lamp at his head, but he deflected the blow with his left arm, shattering the porcelain vase and crumpling the shade. Then, he brought the knife down in a savage plunge.

Teresa gasped as sharp pain flooded her being. The knife had slid into her side and by the time the killer pulled it out, red blossomed on the white sheets.

She held up her hands to ward off another blow, a plea for her life on her lips but no breath to give it a voice, and then the knife came down again, spattering the headboard and drapes of Patrick's dad's motorhome with arterial spray.

The second period bell rang shrilly through the hallways of Crimson Bay High as classroom doors opened and students spilled out.

In a graffiti-scrawled cubicle in the girls' bathroom, Lauren Mackenzie palmed away the last of her tears and tried to compose herself. It was the first day back at school and already she wasn't able to keep it together. Was this year really going to be as bad as the last one? She didn't think that was remotely possible, but it sure looked like it was giving it a shot.

It had been Tommy Graziano who had made the wisecrack that had sent her running to the bathroom in tears. And he wasn't even one of the nasty kids. It was just a dumb joke and Lauren knew she could expect much worse from some of the others. But it was on everybody's mind. The question, the titillating curiosity, the weird sense of the past repeating itself.

Had her father returned?

It wasn't easy growing up in a small town where your father was, quite literally, the local boogeyman. She hadn't even known herself until seventh grade. She had grown up under a different name, a name she still carried like a disguise. But everybody knew. Everybody knew she was the daughter Anthony Stevens, convicted child molester and mass murderer. Anthony Stevens, who had broken out of jail and come back to his hometown to claim the lives of eleven victims. Anthony Stevens, who had been shot by the police and vanished into the woods. Anthony Stevens, whose body had never been recovered.

Lauren knew he was dead. The events of that night were etched into her brain like a burning brand. She had flung herself to the dirt as Sheriff Weiss had identified himself. She had squeezed her eyes shut as the gunshots had rung out in the still night air. She hadn't opened them until the sheriff had placed his hand on her, telling her that *he* was gone, that it was over.

But it hadn't been over. It would never be over. Anthony Stevens – her father – was dead but, as no corpse had been found, there had been no closure for the families of the victims. No closure for Lauren. There would always be that little doubt that he was dead, just enough to blame every creepy or unexplained thing on.

Like the brutal murder of a couple in their motorhome parked on Mount Lenzi, barely yards away from where Anthony Stevens had committed his most gruesome murders five years before.

It was the most horrific thing to have happened in the county since that night and, if it wasn't the work of Stevens having returned to his old stomping ground, then it was a hell of a coincidence. Or perhaps some sick copycat.

And that had been the basis of Tommy Graziano's joke which he aimed at Lauren at the end of first period math. Something about her father having a 'fan club'. She didn't know why she let herself get so upset by this bullshit. It wasn't like it was anything new. She'd had to deal with gibes and sick remarks more or less constantly over the past five years. After it became common knowledge who she really was, it was like it was open season on her. People seemed to forget the little fact that Anthony Stevens had murdered her mom and the man she had grown up believing was her dad too.

And now another poor couple had been murdered. Brutally stabbed to death and left naked, either stripped and raped by the killer or butchered while getting it on (the papers were a little hazy on that point). Didn't that call for a little taste and respect? Why did everything have to become some big joke at her expense?

The bathroom door slammed open, and Lauren instinctively drew her knees up to her chin so nobody could spot her grubby Converse All Stars underneath the stall. A gaggle of voices filled the room, echoing off the cracked tiles and mold-flecked ceiling.

"My dad is basically convinced that I'm gonna get murdered as soon as I step out the front door," a girl's voice said. "So I'm basically under house arrest apart from going to school."

"Mine's the same," said another girl. "Did you get the talk about coming straight home after school?"

"Big time. Jeez, it's like we're in seventh grade again!"

"At least your parents give a fuck," said a third voice. "Mine probably wouldn't even notice if I dropped off the face of the planet."

Oh, great, thought Lauren, recognizing the voice of Brooke McKenna, just about the closest thing she had to a mortal enemy. The other two voices belonged to Valerie Michaels and Jackie Hunter, Brooke's usual partners in crime.

"So, Val," Brooke asked. "Still got the hots for Jeff Duvall?"

"Yeah, he's just too cute!"

"As if! His underbite looks like it could take a chunk out of somebody."

"Well, *I* think he's cute."

"Isn't he still dating Zoe Jordan?" Jackie asked.

"Not for long," Valerie replied. "They're on the skids. They had a massive fight over the summer."

"And Val is waiting on the sidelines for when they split up!" said Brooke and the three girls laughed.

"Maybe that's true," said Valerie. "Just don't tell anybody! Jeez, I would die if people thought I was waiting around for him to ditch her!"

"Come on," said Brooke. "Let's get out of here."

"Wait up," said Valerie. "I need to pee."

Lauren jumped as the door to the stall next to hers slammed open.

"Gross!" Valerie said. "Don't people flush?"

Lauren sat in petrified terror as Valerie tried the door to her stall next.

"Hey, who's in there?" Valerie said. "Have you been listening to us?"

"Come out, we know somebody's in there!" said Brooke, followed by a loud fist pounding on the door. "Do you think hiding your feet can fool us?"

Lauren stuck her fingers in her ears, wishing they would just disappear. The whole row of cubicles started to shake as Brooke hauled herself up to peer over the top of the stall.

"Lauren *Stevens*!" she said triumphantly as her frizzy head gazed down at Lauren. There was an extra emphasis on the last word which wasn't Lauren's surname, legal or otherwise. "Have you been listening to us, you freak?"

Two more heads appeared next to Brooke's.

"You better not tell anybody what you heard," said Valerie.

"Yeah, you tell anybody and you're dead!" said Jackie Hunter.

"Oh, she won't," said Brooke with a sadistic grin. "If she knows what's good for her. Anyway, she's probably too busy thinking up ways to kill people to please her psycho father. Haven't you heard that they're in it together? Like father like daughter, huh?"

Brooke had an especial dislike of Lauren because her big sister had been slain by Anthony Stevens. The late Jill McKenna was thought of as something of a local saint. She had been one of the seniors who had accompanied the ninth grader bicycle trip up Mount Lenzi. The story was that it had been Jill who had led Anthony Stevens away from the ninth graders and had been murdered while they made their escape down the mountain. She had basically given her life to save the younger students and Lauren had decided long ago that if Jill had been a saint, then Brooke had fallen extremely far from the tree.

"Who's next, Lauren?" Brooke asked. "Why don't you do the world a favor and kill yourself instead?"

The other girls laughed and, following Brooke's lead, slipped down from the top of the door.

"You know, the janitor in this place is so fucking lazy," Brooke said. "He never empties the trash until it's completely full. Let's give him a hand."

Lauren had only a moment to comprehend the implications of her words before the three girls reappeared at the top of the cubical, this time bearing one of the trash cans between them. Hoisting it up onto the top of the door, they tipped it over and Lauren gasped in horrified disgust as its contents rained down on her.

Brooke and her friends laughed as tissues, apple cores, banana peels, snack wrappers and even used tampons practically filled the cubical up to Lauren's knees, sticking to her hair and piling up on her shoulders.

"Now the janitor can take her out with the rest of the garbage!" said Brooke, as the three bullies slipped down from the door. Their shrill laughter carried out into the hallway beyond as they left the bathroom.

Lauren waited until the door slammed shut before she dared move in case they got any more ideas. Then, fresh tears streaming down her face, she began brushing the garbage off her, nearly retching at the stink and the unidentifiable liquid that dribbled down her neck.

She unlocked the cubical door and stumbled out, sobbing. She turned on the faucet and splashed her face with cold water, scrubbing at it to remove the stink of refuse that seemed to cling to her. She looked up into the mirror and tried her best to tidy herself up.

Lauren had a pale complexion with light freckles and black hair which always seemed to be greasy no matter how often she washed it. She usually wore it in loose bunches on either side of her neck. She often wore baggy sweaters which hid her figure and, if anybody paid much attention to her, then she would strike them as a girl who wanted to hide from the world. She had no friends and always scurried about with her arms folded, eyes on the ground. Five years of being tripped, shoved and otherwise tormented had made her try her best to be invisible.

Some pink bubblegum had got stuck to the end of her hair and she ripped at it savagely, ignoring the pain as several strands of hair were plucked loose. She still smelled of garbage and there was a stain on the shoulder of her sweater. She tugged it off and tied it around her middle, wincing at the glare of her white t-shirt which bared her arms and showed her small breasts. She never just wore a t-shirt, and it wasn't exactly t-shirt weather in any case. She'd just have to cope and hope that it didn't give anybody yet another thing to comment on.

Running her fingers through her hair to remove any other small bits of crap, she guessed it was as good as it was going to get, and she headed off for second period Geography, head down, hoping nobody would notice the stink.

CHAPTER 3

Lauren did her best to steer clear of everybody for the rest of the day, the stink of garbage still in her nostrils, not sure if it was her imagination or not. It was best to keep a safe distance, just in case but, at the end of lunchtime, Harriet Lipstadt came over to where she was sitting alone in the cafeteria, looking thoroughly reluctant at having to do so.

"Uh, Lauren?" she asked.

"Yeah?"

"I know it's your week to have the car, but could I please just borrow it this afternoon? Mike, Jeff and Zoe and some of the others are going to the movies later and you know my parents won't let me walk home alone after dark with … you know … all that's going on."

"Can't you get a lift with anyone?"

"No, they all live on the other side of town."

Lauren had been living with the Lipstadts for the past five years, ever since Anthony Stevens had killed her parents. The Lipstadts had been friends of the family and were keen to do a good turn by taking her in. Lauren was grateful because it sure beat foster care, but Harriet Lipstadt, despite being in the same grade as Lauren, was anything but receptive to the idea of a new foster sister.

Harriet was OK, not a bully like Brooke McKenna, but Lauren always got the feeling that she would rather be dead than be seen in her company. She wouldn't even ride to school with her, instead settling for a one week on/one week off agreement concerning the Lipstadt's second car; a ten-year-old Chevrolet Caprice with horrible wood paneling along the sides. Lauren was an embarrassment. A family charity case, nothing more. If it wasn't for sharing a roof and the car, then the two girls really wouldn't have had much to do with each other.

"Sure, I guess," Lauren sighed, not really wanting to give up one of her afternoons with the car and hoof it all the way home, but she had always felt a little guilty about intruding on Harriet's family and taking a share in everything that was rightfully hers, including the family car. "I don't think it's going to rain, in any case. I can walk home."

"Thanks."

Lauren pulled the keys out of her pocket and passed them to Harriet, conscious of Harriet's gaggle of popular friends a couple of tables over, sharing a joke and glancing in their direction.

"Oh, and Lauren?" Harriet said, in a low, conspiratorial voice so as not to be overheard.

"Yeah?"

"Take a shower tonight, huh? You stink of garbage."

It was a gray, depressing afternoon as Lauren walked home. Rain threatened but held back in great boiling clouds. She walked with her head down as she aways did, hugging her bare arms, her backpack slung over one shoulder and her sweater still tied around her middle. She wished she could put it on. Her eyes were focused on the sidewalk a few feet in front of her, watching the circles of gum, squashed cigarette butts and cracks in the asphalt pass by.

She became aware of a car slowly creeping along the curb behind her. Her heart started jumping and she grew afraid to turn around. Out of the corner of her eye, she saw the front end of a police cruiser as it slowly rolled past her and came to a stop. Her heart rate slowed. It was just Sheriff Weiss.

"Hi there, Lauren," the sheriff said as he opened the driver's door and got out. "How are you keeping?"

It wasn't the first time Sheriff Weiss had checked in on Lauren. She guessed he felt some sort of connection to her having been the one who had saved her life by shooting Anthony Stevens that awful night five years ago. That and the fact that he had lost his wife to Stevens's blade. She supposed he thought that made them compadres of some sort. If he did, then he was the only person in Crimson Bay who felt that way.

"I'm good, Sheriff," she replied, keeping her eyes on the buckle of his belt which dug into the soft belly of middle age and too much scotch. Sheriff Weiss was approaching fifty, graying at the sides and balding in the middle. People said that he'd aged twice as fast in the past five years which wasn't surprising given that his wife had died in his arms after being brutally stabbed by Lauren's father.

"Good. That's good," he said. "Listen, I guess you heard about that couple up at the picnic ground on Mount Lenzi?"

"Yeah, everybody at school is talking about it."

"Right. Awful business. Look, I just wanted to check in on you, make sure you were OK. Don't go out after dark, huh? Stay indoors and make sure the doors are locked, that sort of thing."

"Is there something I should be worried about, Sheriff?"

"Well, you know, we haven't caught the guy who killed those campers, so it pays to be extra cautious."

Lauren doubted that Sheriff Weiss was advising everybody to lock their doors and avoid going out after dark, so why was she getting the lecture? Did he seriously think it was her father, still alive and killing after all these years?

"Well, give my best to the Lipstadts," the sheriff said before getting back into his cruiser.

"I will, Sheriff. Bye."

"Goodbye, Lauren. Say, why don't you put your sweater on? It looks like rain."

Lauren said nothing and watched the police cruiser head off down the street. As soon as she got home, she took a hot shower and rinsed the last of the garbage smell off her. When she was done, she went downstairs, toweling her wet hair. Mrs. Lipstadt was fixing dinner in the kitchen.

"Oh, hi, Lauren," she said as she chopped vegetables. "I didn't hear you come in. Good day?"

"Sure, Mrs. Lipstadt," she lied, opening the refrigerator to grab a Pepsi.

"I wish you could call me Anne, Lauren," Mrs. Lipstadt chided. "I'm not asking you to call me 'Mom' or anything. But I thought we might be on personal names after five years?"

"Yes, Mrs. Lipst ... uh, *Anne*."

Anne smiled.

The doorbell rang.

"I'll get it," said Lauren. She went out into the hallway and opened the door to find Mrs. Lutz from next door. "Oh, hello, Mrs. Lutz," she said.

"Hi, Lauren, I'm glad I caught you. It's you I came to see, in fact. Would you be able to babysit Corey this Friday?"

Corey was Mrs. Lutz's ten-year-old kid she had been left with after her husband ran off with some other woman. Corey was OK but a bit of a handful at times. He seemed to have taken a liking to Lauren which made him just about the only person in Crimson Bay who had. Even the other parents treated her with a nervous detachment and Corey Lutz was the only babysitting gig she could get.

"I wouldn't ask unless I was absolutely desperate," Mrs. Lutz went on, confirming Lauren's suspicions that, given the choice, *she* wouldn't want the daughter of a mass murder babysitting her kid either, "but I have to work the graveyard shift. You can sleep over, and I'll leave money for a pizza."

"That's fine, Mrs. Lutz," Lauren said.

"Oh, that's wonderful! Thank you so much! Friday at nine, then?"

"Sure."

Lauren closed the door and went back into the kitchen.

"Babysitting that Lutz boy again?" Mrs. Lipstadt asked, still chopping vegetables.

"Friday night," Lauren replied.

"I thought you might have plans, being a Friday and all. A date or something."

The little twinkle in Mrs. Lipstadt's eye told Lauren that she was half-kidding but there was no mockery there. Only mild teasing.

"Hardly," Lauren said.

"Oh, I think you should go out with boys," Mrs. Lipstadt went on. "It would be good for you. For your confidence, you know?"

"Yeah, um. I've got some homework to do so I'll be in my room."

Lauren rolled her eyes as she headed upstairs. *A date? Really?* Mrs. Lipstadt meant well but she was woefully uninformed of just how much of a social pariah her foster daughter really was.

Sheriff Weiss couldn't stop thinking about Lauren Mackenzie as he drove over to the station house. There was something about that kid that just made him sad. Perhaps it was the way she always walked, head down, arms looking like they wanted to carry herself away from everything. Or it was perhaps that he never saw her with any friends.

He wasn't oblivious to the way the whole town treated her and it wouldn't surprise him if she was the victim of bullying at school. After all, Crimson Bay had been wounded so badly five years ago, it took more than a generation to heal that sort of thing. He'd seen the graffiti around town; ugly names and stick figures of father and daughter holding bloody knives. There'd even been a 'Die Lauren Stevens' accompanied with the image of a noose spraypainted on the rear wall of the public library. He'd personally seen to it that that one was removed quickly before the poor kid got to hear of it and he wasn't sure he had succeeded.

Even the adults were still pretty messed up about it all. Take the wife of the late Deputy Johnson for example. Her husband had died on his watch and, while Jeannie said that she forgave him, he had never really been able to forgive himself. Johnson had been a young transfer from Trinity County. A nice guy and a good cop, he'd not been with the department more than six months. On that night, five years ago, Sheriff Weiss had taken little Lauren Mackenzie to his home after her parents had been butchered by Anthony Stevens. He'd put Deputy Johnson on watch in his cruiser outside while he'd gone looking for Stevens. But Stevens had come to the house and butchered both Deputy Johnson and Sheriff Weiss's wife before kidnapping Lauren and taking her up to his old house in the woods.

That night held a stranglehold on Sheriff Weiss's life. He had failed to protect his wife and the life of a damn fine deputy, but he supposed it was worse for Jeannie and the kids who had barely moved in. They had struggled with his death, both financially and emotionally with Jeannie forced to take night work as a cleaner. It was hard on the kids and their son Toby was fast becoming a little punk, rebelling against everything and dressing like it was Halloween all year round.

He hoped the kid wasn't going off the deep end with the occult stuff. Crimson Bay had its share of satanic graffiti to go along with the slander against Lauren Mackenzie. Pentagrams and inverted crosses along with '666' could be seen spraypainted in the derelict areas like the tract of land that ran behind the suburbs where the woods started. He'd even been notified of a dead dog found there that looked like it had been skinned, though the thing was so far gone it was hard to tell. The department had invited an expert on the occult to give them all the low-down on what to look for if a satanic cult was suspected of operating in their jurisdiction. Sheriff Weiss didn't think one was, most likely it was just bored kids fooling around. He just hoped that Toby Johnson wasn't involved.

He guessed the poor kid couldn't be blamed too much, growing up without a dad and his mom's new lowlife of a boyfriend was hardly an ideal role model. Howard DeAngelo was some hard-drinking, ex-con bastard she had picked up at the roadhouse on one of her nights off when the loneliness of being a widow had got too much for her. All Sheriff Weiss knew was that Howard DeAngelo was a poor substitute for Deputy Johnson.

And as if the likes of the Johnson family and Lauren Mackenzie didn't have enough problems, now the past was being raked up again by fresh murders. He couldn't figure it. The two campers had been out of towners, shacking up together for a weekend. The brutality with which they had been butchered was all too reminiscent of the crimes of Anthony Stevens, but it had been five years, goddamn it! He had shot Stevens himself after following him up to that old house where he had taken Lauren. Sure, he had limped away into the woods and had never been seen again, but with three bullets in him? He *had* to be dead.

Sheriff Weiss was convinced that whoever had killed those campers was somebody new. Perhaps somebody from out of town with a motive as yet unascertained. Maybe they knew the campers. And yet, there were no other tire tracks near the vehicle. It was like the killer had come out of nowhere. Had somebody *walked* up the side of Mount Lenzi just to kill them? The only evidence of activity was a burned-out campfire on the peak of the mountain, still warm the morning after. *Somebody* had been up there all right. And Sheriff Weiss was determined to find out who.

CHAPTER 4

Toby turned up the volume on his stereo, which was already blasting out Merciful Fate, to block out the yelling downstairs. His stepdad, Howard, was home from work and that meant the atmosphere in the house changed like flipping on a switch. He was tearing into Toby's mother about some damn thing which was more than a frequent occurrence. Whatever. As long as he left Toby and his little sister alone, that's all Toby cared about.

As far as he was concerned, Mom had known Howard was a loser when she brought him home from that roadhouse, so she could deal with the consequences. Anyway, he was heading out soon so they could yell at each other all they wanted. It wasn't like he had anywhere important to be, but anything was better than hanging around this dump.

He had agreed to meet Brooke, Todd and Gary over at the park. No big plans, just hanging out. Todd could always lift a few beers from his dad and Gary usually had weed on him. That was the only thing those guys were good for. He only hung out with them because it meant he could hang out with Brooke, but she insisted on dating that loser, Todd. She was way too good for him and didn't even realize it.

He had done all he could to turn her attention towards him and bring down calamity on Todd but nothing ever worked. He had tried the Invocation Employed Towards the Conjuration of Destruction from *The Satanic Bible*, called on every demonic being to do his will and even stuck pins in a wax figurine but nothing terrible ever happened to Todd. As for Brooke, he had tried to conjure her lust in every conceivable way, using satanic rituals to invoke Pan, burning candles and jerking off to a polaroid of her propped up on his homemade satanic altar.

It was a polaroid her friend Valerie had taken last summer but Brooke had hated it and tossed it in the trash at the end of recess. Toby had plucked it out when nobody had been looking and taken it home with him. He didn't understand why she didn't like it. It had been taken at the corny old funfair which came to Crimson Bay every summer and Brooke had been sitting at a table with the horses of the carousel in the background. Her curly hair hung down over one shoulder and the way she was sitting made her red and white t-shirt stretch just slightly across her boobs. Toby loved that picture, and he loved Brooke.

He took the polaroid off his homemade altar and put it back in his nightstand drawer along with the box of Kleenex. The altar was little more than a stool painted black beneath a large, inverted pentagram he had painted on his wall, surrounded by posters of his favorite bands – Venom, Merciful Fate and Slayer among others – long-haired ghouls in black leather and studs along with various satanic images.

He was beginning to lose interest in the whole occult thing. Maybe it *was* all just an image to sell records like some people said. Nothing seemed to work anyway. Not spells or invocations. It was all just words. Even that weird translation of a medieval satanic monk he had spent days studying and preparing for had turned out to be a crock of shit. He glanced at the notebook Gary had loaned him. As the one member of the group who had an interest in the occult, it had been his job to make it all feel authentic. But that's all it had turned out to be. Set dressing and make believe like the movies. It shouldn't have surprised him that the medieval monk's scribblings had turned out to be fake, just like everything else in life. Perhaps there really was nothing more to life than the pursuit of getting wasted and laid in an endless cycle until you died.

Feeling even more depressed than usual, he pulled on his denim jacket and headed downstairs where Howard was still yelling at his mom. His little sister, Cathy, was watching cartoons in the living room and he ruffled her hair as he passed, hoping to slip out the front door without being noticed.

"Where the hell do you think you're going?" Howard demanded from the kitchen.

Toby sighed. "Out."

"On a Monday? You done your homework?"

"Why the hell do you care?"

"Oh, you're gonna start with that attitude?" Howard came storming out of the kitchen. He wasn't any taller than Toby but had a compact body from years of manual labor and his forearms were knotted with muscle beneath his rolled-up shirt sleeves. "Jesus, what the fuck do you look like?" he continued, apparently bored with berating his girlfriend and keen to make a start on Toby. "Are you wearing make-up again? You embarrass your mother by going out dressed like a goddamned fag, you know that?"

"Fuck off, *Howard*," Toby said, flicking him the bird.

He turned to leave but Howard grabbed him by the shoulders and spun him around. The fist hit him in the solar plexus like a jackhammer, doubling him over. He heard his mom scream as the wind was knocked from him and he sank to his knees. "Don't hurt him, Howard!" she wailed from the kitchen.

He didn't listen. The right hook caught Toby just below the eye and sent him sprawling to the carpet, his head ringing. He heard the distant cries of his little sister, and he hated this bastard more than ever.

"You're too lenient on these brats, Jeannie," Howard said, standing triumphantly over Toby who writhed at his feet. "Maybe their old man was too. I would have thought a cop would know how to discipline his kids."

If Toby had had the strength left in him, he would have lunged at Howard for talking about his father that way. But he could barely get to his feet and by the time he had done that, Howard had walked away and had his head in the refrigerator, rootling about for a beer.

Toby couldn't remain in the house a moment longer and stumbled out the front door, slamming it behind him.

Gary ignored the framed photograph of his mom in her gym coach's attire on the shelf as he raided the small wooden box above the TV for loose change. Dad had started keeping a little deposit of dollar bills in there and when Gary was desperate, he sometimes helped himself, always making sure to leave a few bills behind. He doubted if Dad knew how much he had squirreled away in any case. It wasn't like he didn't leave Gary pizza money when he was staying late at school or off visiting his lame new girlfriend, but Gary's habits tended to be on the expensive side.

Taking a few bills without bothering to count them, he stuffed them into his jeans pocket and then headed into the kitchen for something to eat. Finding two leftover slices of pizza, he ate one with the refrigerator door open and then took the other with him.

He munched on the last slice of cold pizza as he locked up the house and headed up the street. He went out most nights. He couldn't remember the last time he and Dad had eaten dinner together. Gary pretty much lived off leftovers and cereal and had the house to himself most of the time.

As an only kid with a dead mom and a father who was more interested in throwing himself into his work and the arms of dorky women, the house didn't exactly ring with the sound of family. Pictures of Mom still cluttered the shelves, and the upstairs closet was still stuffed with her clothes. He guessed all that would change once Dad plucked up the courage to start bringing Suzanne back here. As it was, the house was a snapshot of happier times with all the people removed except him. His dad seemed content to leave it all be and pursue another life in motels and the back of Suzanne's crappy camper. But Gary still had to live in the ruins of their former life.

He never dwelled on these thoughts for long and spent as little time in the gloomy house as he could. There were always people to see, stuff to do. Like hanging with his buddy Hal who lived at the end of the street.

Hal Griffin was twenty-three and a total wastiod who sat around all day smoking reefers in the back of his garage which was cluttered with half-assembled dirt bikes. He claimed to make a living as a mechanic and occasionally tooled around with one for a paying customer but anybody who really knew him had an idea where the bulk of his income came from.

A small town like Crimson Bay didn't boast a huge number of drug dealers and, as far as the kids of Crimson Bay High were concerned, Hal Griffin had cornered the market. Hal could get you anything; weed, uppers, downers, even cocaine for those who could afford it.

Gary never knocked on the front door. Hal was always in the garage with the door rolled down, sealing in the fug of weed smoke. He hammered on the side door and waited.

"Gary, my man!" said the tall, shaggy-haired creature who opened the door. "Get your ass in here, before the cops smell my stash downtown."

Gary stepped in and Hal shut the door behind them. The place was practically wall to wall with smoke and they flopped down on an old couch in front of a TV set Hal had rigged up amid the clutter of his bike repair operation.

"So, what's the word on the street, my man?" Hal said as he passed Gary an open bag of potato chips.

"Oh, you know," Gary said, accepting the bag and digging in hungrily. "School shit. Home shit. *Same* old shit."

"You hear about that couple who got sliced and diced up on Mount Lenzi?"

Gary nodded as he munched potato chips.

"Brings back bad memories, man. For you too, I guess. Sorry for bringing it up. I mean, I knew three of those kids who got killed way back then. They were in my class, but you ... your mom, I mean."

"Yeah."

"Sorry, man."

"No problem. Look, can I get a few grams? I'm hanging out with some people later and they always like to blaze up."

"Sure, man, anytime. What do you need?"

"How much can you give me for this?" he reached into his jeans pocket and pulled out the scrunched-up wad of notes.

Hal took the cash and riffled through it, his usually befuddled mind suddenly clear when it came to the cash-to-ounce ratio. "I can let you have half an ounce, and that's for a buddy."

He got up and, taking a key from his pocket, took down a small cash box from a high shelf, opened it and tossed in Gary's money. Then he opened a rusty old tool chest and took out a mason jar stuffed with bags of weed. Plucking one out, he tossed it to Gary.

"None of that Mexican ditch weed either," he said. "This is Panama Red, my man."

Gary opened the little plastic baggie and sniffed the contents, a wide smile spreading across his face.

"Believe me," said Hal, "that shit will take your mind off anything."

"Perfect," said Gary, pocketing the baggie.

Dinner at the McKenna household was usually a somber and silent affair. Cutlery clicked against crockery as the three of them ate their pork chops and asparagus without saying a word to each other. They always ate quickly, like it was a chore to get through. Then each of them would go their separate ways; Brooke to her room or out, her dad to his TV set in the den and her mom to bed more often than not. Three people who lived together, but nothing resembling a family. Not anymore.

Brooke glanced at Jill's seat. Nobody referred to it as 'Jill's seat', but it was where she had used to sit, and nobody had sat there for five years. It wasn't like her parents still set a place for her at dinner or anything like that (even her parents weren't *that* messed up), but it was still Jill's seat, nonetheless, always vacant, always unspoken of. Her bedroom had remained untouched since her death, and it was the dull, black heart of the house that no longer beat. Jill had always been their parents' favorite and now that they had lost her, Brooke's presence in their lives was barely noticed.

41

"Awful business about those campers," said her father suddenly, as he got his mouth around a forkful of asparagus.

Brooke and her mom looked at him like he had sprouted wings. *Nobody* spoke during dinner. Never.

"Probably some out of towner," he continued while he munched.

"The world is a godawful place," Brooke's mom said thoughtfully as she gazed at her glass of wine.

"Stabbed to death, apparently," her dad said. "Sheriff Weiss will have his hands full with the press unless he can catch the killer quickly." He carved off a piece of pork chop and shoved it in his mouth before continuing to talk. "Whole state will have its eye on Crimson Bay now. After ... you know, its history."

"*Must* you state the absolute obvious?" Brooke's mom said, shooting him a withering stare.

"Just making conversation," he replied innocently.

"Well, I think we could all do without *that* sort of conversation at the dinner table."

Brooke looked at the clock on the wall. A quarter to six. She sighed. Todd had been given detention by Mrs. Ross for goofing off in physics. *Dumb ape.* They had planned to hit the mall after school, eat a hamburger and fool around at the arcade for an hour or two before hooking up with Gary and Toby at the park. Valerie and Jackie's parents weren't letting them out of their sight and, with Todd stuck at school, she had been forced to come home which was the most depressing place in the world.

The horn of Todd's van blared outside, and Brooke nearly gasped in relief. He had come, like a chubby knight in rusty armor to save her from the miserable tedium of her parents.

They both looked at her in surprise, as if noticing her for the first time in five years. "Where are you going?" her mother asked as she stood up.

"Out with Todd," Brooke replied.

"When there's a killer out there?" her mom said incredulously. "Oh, no. You're staying in after dark from now on, young lady."

"You're kidding," said Brooke, genuinely astonished. Her mom hadn't laid the law down about anything since Jill's death. Most of the time she was too doped up on prescription drugs to care what her youngest daughter got up to.

"Didn't you hear anything your father and I discussed?" her mom said. "There's another killer out there and I'm not losing another daughter to some psycho!"

"Evelyn, don't you think you might be overreacting?" said her dad. "We can't keep Brooke locked up like some sort of prisoner. She's going out with Todd. She'll be perfectly safe."

"How can you be so flippant about your daughter's safety?" her mom demanded. "I would have thought that you'd at least back me up on this!"

"I just don't think we should allow ourselves to be held hostage by whoever this person is. Life must be allowed to go on as normal otherwise the killer wins."

"So you'll sacrifice your own daughter's life just for some silly philosophy!" her mom shrieked.

"Calm down, Evelyn ..."

"I will *not* calm down!"

Brooke got up and left them to it. They didn't even notice her go out into the hall and put on her jacket. They had quickly forgotten her as another fight consumed them.

There was the sound of breaking crockery as she slipped out the front door. Her mom had not had these violent fits for a couple of years now. Dr. Donahue had put her on some pretty good meds which kept her docile. Tonight she was kicking off like it was for old times' sake.

Todd was waiting in his Dodge van, arm hanging out the window, cigarette between his fingers. "Hey, babe," he called. "What's all the ruckus? I can hear your folks from here."

"Those assholes are at each other's throats again," said Brooke as she came around to the passenger's side and got in. "What time did you get away?"

"Fucking bitch kept me 'til five! She's really got it in for me. If I fail physics, my dad said he'll get me a job in his goddamned factory. Fucking game over."

"You got out at five and you're only picking me up now?" Brooke seethed.

He shrugged. "I was hungry and needed to grab some beers from home."

"You could have picked me up first. I had to sit through another dinner from hell because of you!"

"Hey, lighten up, babe," he said, reaching out to stroke her chin.

She turned her head from his touch, more violently than she had intended.

"Wow, I'm sorry, OK?" Todd said as he revved the engine and pulled away from the curb.

Brooke said nothing. Sometimes she wondered why she was with Todd. It wasn't like he turned her on or anything. He was a tubby, crude oaf who took pride in his belches and had the intellect of a wet mop. But he was into her and had a van besides. It was also something to do, somebody to be with.

She had hoped her parents would sternly disapprove, but when they didn't seem to care, it only made her angrier and she even found herself resenting Todd for not being dangerous enough to earn their ire.

44

She let him ride her in the back of his van; clumsy, sweaty sessions that never lasted long enough to really bother her, but they had grown few and far between of late. She didn't know if that was his doing or hers. It didn't *seem* like he was losing interest in her, but she knew that she had lost interest in him long ago.

They cruised through benighted suburbia with the volume turned up on Todd's battered AC/DC cassette, the windows rolled down just to piss off the whole neighborhood. He gripped the wheel with one hand and took swigs from a can of beer in the other while alternating between belches and bad renditions of the chorus to 'You Shook Me All Night Long'. Brooke wondered once again why she was with him.

CHAPTER 5

Brooke and Todd headed for the park, though that was a generous word for the square of scrubland containing a few vandalized pieces of jungle gym equipment and graffiti-streaked benches left there a couple of decades ago in an attempt to make the area attractive for families. It was right on the edge of town where the suburbs petered out into the woods which rose up the slope of Mount Lenzi, cut across by the highway. Between the park and the highway was a wooded dip where people had tossed all sorts of junk over the years; tires, busted refrigerators and other detritus which made an even better playground for the bored youth of Crimson Bay. Todd, Brooke, Toby and Gary often came here to shoot Todd's BB gun at glass bottles or just lounge around drinking and smoking.

Toby was already there when they pulled up, sitting atop a rusty old refrigerator, looking even gloomier than usual. There was a big purple bruise around his left eye.

"What happened to you, Johnson?" Todd asked as they approached.

"My asshole stepdad," said Toby, glancing up.

"Fuck, I thought my dad was a bastard," said Todd, poking Toby's bruise with a forceful finger.

"Ow, watch it, asshole!" Toby yelled angrily.

"Don't be such a pussy!" said Todd.

Gary arrived, hands thrust into his denim jacket pockets, woolen hat pulled low.

"Here comes our candy man," said Brooke.

"Hey, man," Todd said, nodding at Gary. "You got some funky stuff for us?"

"Of course," Gary replied, pulling a plastic baggie out of his jacket pocket.

They sat down, cracked open some beers and watched Gary roll an impressive joint. It was fully dark now and the only light came from the flickering streetlights up on the highway and the moon behind drifting clouds. They smoked, drank and cracked jokes. One thing they did not discuss was last week's black magic session on top of the mountain. It had been a failure and each of them felt a little foolish, like they were afraid the others thought they had been too invested in it. Of course it had all been bullshit and the notebook Gary had stolen from his dad's girlfriend lay somewhere in Toby's bedroom, forgotten.

Toby was even more sullen and silent than usual. He possibly felt more foolish than the rest of them, being the 'occult guy' and all. It wasn't as if he was on a steady footing with the others in any case. They let him hang around and shoot the shit with them but none of the other three considered him a friend and, if any of them stopped to think about it, they wouldn't be able to pinpoint how or when he had started hanging out with them. It had been Gary who had introduced him to the group at some point but even Gary didn't know him all that well. Nobody did. Toby was a world apart from most at Crimson Bay High and he had no other friends. He just sort of started lurking around the other three like a shadow that they tolerated.

Brooke sat with her back to the woods, and inhaled deeply from the joint as it was passed around. Tears sprung from her eyes as the burning smoke filled her lungs. "Jesus Christ!" she hissed as she passed the joint on.

Gary grinned manically. "Good shit, huh? Panama Red, the best there is!"

As Brooke exhaled, a noise like the snapping of a twig behind her made her jump and she began to cough violently, the smoke caught in her windpipe.

"Take it easy, Brooke!" laughed Gary. "You're supposed to let it relax you."

Brooke could barely talk but she kept looking behind her as she tried to get her breathing back under control. "You guys ..." *cough!* "... hear that?" she gasped.

"Hear what?" Todd said, his eyes half closed as he sucked in a drag.

"Something in the woods behind us. Animal or something."

"Don't let this shit get you paranoid," said Gary.

"I definitely heard something ..." Brooke said as she continued looking over her shoulder. The wind was making the branches waver and the deep darkness between the trees was suddenly unsettling, especially with the recent news that a killer might be out there once again. She shivered and told herself to take Gary's advice. *Don't get paranoid.* But the more she looked into those shadows, the more she felt like something was looking back at her.

"Uh, guys," she said slowly as her heartrate began to quickly increase. "Are you seeing this?"

"Seeing what?" Toby asked.

"Over there, under the trees," she said. "Doesn't that look like ... I don't know, a *person* standing there?"

"What did I tell you?" said Gary, rolling his eyes. "Paranoid."

"No, wait, man," said Todd, his eyes slowly widening. "She's right, it does look like somebody is standing there."

"Fuck!" said Toby, sliding down from his perch atop the refrigerator.

They could all see it now; the definite outline of a shadowy figure standing just at the tree line, watching them.

"Hey, buddy!" Todd yelled, standing up and doing his macho bit. "You got a problem? What the fuck are you staring at?"

The figure stumbled forward and, as the moonlight hit its face, all four of them leapt up in alarm. A cry of terror escaped from Brooke's lips. The figure seemed to be a man, though there was little left of him to identify him as such. His face was a mess of rotten flesh and shriveled, shrunken skin which pulled back around his mouth to reveal a rictus grin of stained, yellowed teeth. One eye was missing and the other looked to be little more than jelly, but it could apparently see or sense them as it lurched towards them like a drunk.

"Get back!" Todd yelled, his voice quivering.

The four of them kept walking backwards as the creature lumbered on. Gary picked up a rock and hurled it at the creature's head. It split the skin on his scalp and bounced off. The blood didn't run from the cut but oozed slowly, as if already coagulated.

"The thing's a fucking zombie!" Gary hissed. "No way is it alive!"

The creature had been stopped in its tracks by the rock that had injured it. It looked about dumbly, not sure what to do with itself. The four kids stopped walking backwards and just stared at it.

"You don't think ..." said Toby, "this guy has anything to do with ... you know. What we did the other night?"

"You tell us, Grand Wizard!" Todd snapped. "I thought we were supposed to bring back your folks and Brooke's big sister. Who the fuck is this guy?"

"Nobody we knew," said Gary. "But it's a hell of a coincidence. We do a resurrection ritual and this guy shows up?"

"Wait ..." said Toby, creeping closer to the shambling zombie. "Wait just a minute ..."

"Toby, watch out!" Brooke cried.

"I don't think this is one of the victims," Toby continued, examining the creature close up. He peered into the ruined face and then looked over the torn and ragged clothes. "I mean, we've all seen pictures, right. *Of him*. Of when he was put away the first time. And then there were those wanted posters that went around town with the artist's impression of what he looked like the night he vanished. What clothes he was wearing ..."

The other three looked him over, the name on all of their lips left unspoken as if it might suddenly bring the man to his senses. *Anthony Stevens*.

He was wearing the jeans and striped polo shirt that he had taken from his first victim that night he had escaped prison five years ago. The clothes, like the rest of him, looked like they had been buried for a long time. His bony hands were like claws, clutching spasmodically at his sides as if he wasn't quite sure what he was grasping at.

"Jesus," said Todd. "Is it really him?"

"I guess we know who killed those campers," said Gary. "He really did come back, after all."

"I don't think he wants to hurt us," Toby replied. "He's just looking at us, like he wants us to do something."

"Fuck, I'll do something!" Brooke said. Her fear had melted away now to be replaced by a venomous rage. This was the man who had murdered her sister. The guy who had ruined their lives. And when they had tried to bring their loved ones back, this thing returned instead like it was one big joke being played on them. That part made her madder than all the rest and she picked up a broken log and ran towards the thing that had been Anthony Stevens with a scream.

She swung the log at his head as hard as she could. It connected with a sickening crunch and snapped in half, leaving the others wondering if the sound had come from the breaking wood or the caving in of the creature's skull.

His head was knocked to one side, the neck looking like it had been broken but, to their astonishment, he lifted his head back into place with a grinding of vertebrae.

"Holy shit, he can't die!" said Todd helpfully.

"We can have some fun with this bastard," said Gary, picking up a discarded beer bottle. "Hey, creep! You killed my mother, you fucking son of a bitch!" He hurled the bottle at the thing's head, and they all cheered as it smashed against its skull, knocking it back a few paces. "He's not even gonna fight back!" Gary yelled deliriously.

With that knowledge, it became a free-for-all against this thing which had caused them so much pain. Every lousy thing about their lives that they could trace back to the night Anthony Stevens had taken their loved ones from them was visited on him tenfold as they pelted him with objects and whacked him with sticks and lengths of pipe like he was a hellish piñata.

Even Todd got in on the fun, despite having no real grievance against Anthony Stevens. But when he balled up his fist and slammed it into the creature's face, the thing suddenly launched itself at him, locking its hands around his neck, bony fingers digging in deep.

"Help!" Todd gasped, almost pissing himself with fear as the creature began to choke him. "Get it off me!"

The other three grabbed hold of its arms, marveling at its strength and trying to ignore the slippery feel of its rotten flesh under their hands. Todd's face began to turn purple, and Gary picked up a heavy rock and slammed it down on the back of the creature's head, knocking him sprawling with Todd, Toby and Brooke beneath him.

"Get away from me! Get away from me!" Todd howled as he tried to scramble out from under the weight of the creature.

The others hauled it off him and Todd jumped up, rubbing his bruised neck and looking like he was going to be sick. "Why the hell did it go for me and none of you guys?" he whined. "All I did was take a swing at him!"

"You didn't make the sacrifice," said Toby. "You didn't lose anyone and you didn't take part in the ritual."

"Hey, I was there!"

"But you didn't *offer* anything. Maybe we're protected from this thing but you ... You're just another potential victim."

"Keep it away from me!" Todd said, frantically making sure the others were between him and it, as a protective barrier. Toby smiled, thoroughly enjoying Todd's discomfort.

"So, it really is because of us that *he* came back," said Brooke. "The ritual worked. Kind of. But why did it bring *him* back?"

"I don't know," said Toby. "Maybe we misunderstood the ritual."

"Maybe *you* misunderstood it, you mean," said Todd.

"That passage in Sumerian or whatever," said Gary. "Nobody could have understood that. Maybe we didn't understand exactly what we were bringing back. But, whatever, we have our very own zombie now!"

"Let's set the bastard on fire!" said Brooke. "He creeps me out."

"I'm down for that!" said Todd. "I'll get some gasoline from my van."

"No, wait!" Toby protested. "If we burn him to a crisp then he'll be gone for good. We could still have a use for him."

"As what, like a pet?" Todd asked. "You're sicker than I thought, Johnson."

"Not as a pet," Toby said. "As a tool."

"For what?"

"In that notebook you stole from your stepmom, Gary, there was a spell for controlling a summoned revenant. Like a servant."

"You want a zombie servant?" said Brooke.

"A *serial killer* servant," Toby corrected her. "One that will do exactly as we say. Kill who we tell it to kill. A slave that will take the fall for us. Think about it, it's the perfect way to off somebody!"

The other three looked at each other uncertainly. "Uh, who do you want to kill, Toby?" asked Gary."

Toby looked from him to the zombified Anthony Stevens, and a grin spread across his face that chilled the others to the bone. "My fucking stepdad," he said.

CHAPTER 6

Lauren usually carried the trash out after dinner every evening while Mrs. Lipstadt did the dishes. It wasn't exactly that she felt like she had to help out as a way to say thanks for letting her live there, but she had started doing it five years ago when she had moved in with the Lipstadts and it's hard to stop being helpful once you've started.

As she lifted the lid on the garbage can and dumped the trash bag into it, somebody leapt up from behind the fence on the other side, clinging to the top of it so that it bent backwards precariously. A hideous, zombified face glared down at her and she stepped back in alarm, holding the trashcan lid up like a shield.

"Goddamn it, Corey!" she snapped as the figure pulled the rubber mask off its face to reveal the delighted grin of Corey Lutz.

"Gotcha!"

"You know I don't like that kind of thing," Lauren replied. As her nerves began to stop crackling and the flashback to being grabbed from behind by her father as she had looked down on the corpse of Deputy Johnson, blood pumping from the gash in his throat, receded, she felt like telling Corey exactly why she didn't like practical jokes or people leaping out at her. But then, she figured that he was just a young kid. What did he know of her trauma? Besides, she didn't want to give him nightmares by relating her gruesome family history. She guessed he knew that Anthony Stevens was her father – the whole town knew, damn it – but she'd rather spare him the gory details.

"We've got a date this Friday, right?" Corey said, his mask propped on the top of his head.

"If by 'date' you mean I'm babysitting you, then yes, we do," Lauren replied, placing the lid back on the trash can.

"Aw, don't call it that!" Corey moaned. "I'm not a baby. I don't even need somebody coming over to look after me. I look after myself pretty good the rest of the time."

"Well, this one's gonna be an overnighter, buddy. Your mom has the night shift."

"Can we stay up all night?"

"No."

"Can we watch horror movies?"

"No."

"Can we make popcorn?"

"Maybe."

"Hey, you wanna see something freaky?"

"Always," said Lauren with a smile. Corey was seriously into anything weird or unexplained. If he wasn't going on about UFOs or Bigfoot, then it would be some new other craze of his like shrunken heads or snakes or the Bermuda Triangle.

"Follow me!" he said, crooking a finger.

Lauren followed the fence and met Corey in the street that ran behind their houses. He led her to the end of the row where the street petered out into the wooded slopes of Mount Lenzi. An old woman lived at the end of the street, all alone and had the reputation of being the local oddball.

"Poor old Mrs. Wallace," Mr. Lipstadt had said one time. "Lost her mind a few years back. Still, it can't be healthy living all alone like that."

Mrs. Wallace could often be seen pottering around in her garden or sitting by her window, watching the birds. Nobody ever saw her in town because she had her groceries delivered but nobody seemed to know anything about her family or, at least, nobody in town owned up to being related to her. She was a frail-looking old bird, with white, wispy hair and always wore rubber boots with her old, floral dresses, whatever the weather was doing.

As Lauren and Corey approached her yard, they could see her standing just by the tree line, staring into the woods as if in a trance. She was mumbling to herself, and Lauren couldn't catch the words over the sighing of the wind in the trees.

"She's been standing like that all afternoon, jabbering away to herself," said Corey. "Weirdo city!"

"That's not funny, Corey," Laren chided. "She's not well." She unlatched the gate and entered the garden. "Mrs. Wallace?" she called.

Mrs. Wallace didn't seem to notice her presence and remained with her back to her, intent on some invisible thing in the woods. As Lauren approached, she was able to make out some of what she was saying.

"Cold ... cold ... always cold at night. Night is when they come. They sing and they dance. Sleep in the day. They know a spell for stealing a cow's face."

"Mrs. Wallace?" said Lauren. She placed a hand on the old woman's shoulder and her bones felt like brittle old twigs beneath her palm.

Mrs. Wallace slowly turned and gazed at Lauren in confusion.

"Are you OK?" Lauren asked.

"You've seen him, haven't you?" the old lady asked.

"Seen who, Mrs. Wallace?"

"He's been sleeping. But now he's awake."

"Would you like me to help you back indoors? I think you've gotten a little confused."

The old lady let Lauren guide her by the hand. Lauren had never been inside Mrs. Wallace's house before. It was a relic from at least two decades ago, all pine and plaid with threadbare carpets and that musty, old person's smell that made Lauren wrinkle her nose. There were masses of junk everywhere; mostly old newspapers and books, stacked up in neat piles. There was something of an ordered chaos to the house. Framed photographs dotted the walls proved that Mrs. Wallace did indeed have a large family, although one long since dispersed.

Lauren helped Mrs. Wallace over to her easy chair by the window where she sat most days.

"He comes at night, only at night," the old lady muttered as she sank down into the chair. "He sleeps in the day. That poor boy. What they did to him ... poor boy, poor boy."

"You just sit there and take it easy," said Lauren. "Is there something I can get you?"

"Poor boy. He is what they made him. But you know that, don't you, Lauren?"

"I'm going to have to go now," Lauren said, surprised that Mrs. Wallace recognized her by name. "Is there anybody you'd like me to call?"

"Poor boy ..."

As she turned to leave, a withered and spotted arm shot out and grasped her by the wrist. "Lauren Stevens!" the old lady hissed.

"Th ... that's not my name ..." Lauren said. She tried to gently pull her arm away, but sharp fingers dug into her flesh with a strength that defied the old woman's weak frame.

"Lauren Stevens ..."

The old woman was leaning forward in her chair, her eyes wide and bloodshot. Lauren could smell sickness on her breath.

"Lauren Stevens ..."

"Please, Mrs. Walters!" Lauren cried. She jerked her hand away, leaving red lines from the old woman's fingernails.

"Lauren Stevens!"

Lauren backed away, leaving the old woman leaning forward in her chair as if she might get up at any moment. But she couldn't stay in that house a moment longer. She backed all the way into the kitchen and then turned and fled, slamming the door shut behind her.

"What's the matter with you?" Corey asked. He'd been hanging around in the garden, inspecting the birdbath.

"Nothing," said Lauren as she tried to compose herself. It was almost dark, and the last golden flare of dusk was settling between the trees on the edge of the property. "Come on, it's late. You'd best get indoors."

CHAPTER 7

Howard left the roadhouse just after closing time. It was raining and he swore as he slipped on the mud just outside, nearly going ass over tip in the process. He was drunk but that never stopped him piling into his pickup and heading home on a weeknight.

He fumbled for his keys and got into the vehicle, revving the engine a little too hard as he left the parking lot, wheels skidding in the mud beneath the neon sign of the roadhouse. Rumbling up onto the highway, he flipped on the radio. The trees swept past as he followed the winding road that led back into town, black shadows and bars of moonlight passing across his dazed face.

He gripped the wheel firmly, keeping an eye on the yellow stripes down the center of the blacktop. He was pretty loaded, and it wouldn't do to get pulled over. Not that there were any cops on the road at this time of night. Sheriff Weiss was probably sitting on his fat ass in the station house instead of getting out and trying to find out who had killed those campers.

Weiss had it in for him, Howard was sure of it. The first time they'd met, he'd grilled him about his past like he was some bum in town that needed moving on. And wouldn't you know it, Weiss already knew about his record? He'd obviously done his homework and Howard knew exactly why. Jeannie had said that he'd been sniffing around her not long after her husband had been killed and she'd had to tell him she wasn't interested. That fat bastard fancied himself in the shoes of the man he'd gotten killed! Some fucking nerve ...

As far Jeannie's lousy kids were concerned, Howard was tempted to wish the man luck, especially that Toby fag with his dyed hair and make-up! But Jeannie was his and, even though they fought often enough to make Howard prefer hitting the roadhouse most nights, he was going to keep her and Sheriff Weiss could go fuck himself.

There was a noise behind him, like something heavy rolling about in the bed of the truck. One glance up into the rearview mirror nearly gave Howard a heart attack. A face was staring back at him through the grimy glass window in the back of the cab. It belonged to a shadowed, hunched figure, just squatting there, peering in.

Howard's jaw dropped and before he could think of pulling over to deal with the lunatic who was hitching a ride, hands smashed through the glass and seized him by the throat. Cold, clammy hands with a wetness to him that made him think of white grubs wriggling in the dirt. But there was a strength to them that made him cry out in pain as broken nails dug into his flesh. There was an awful odor too; a moldering stink of decay that seeped into the cab through the broken window.

The pickup veered wildly, zigzagging across the yellow lines as Howard lost control of the wheel and fought to breathe, tugging and yanking on the hands that gripped him. The truck went off the road, its left headlight smashing against a tree that sent a shuddering jerk through the vehicle, flipping it onto its side. Howard screamed as the vehicle rolled, showering him with broken glass. The awful grip on his throat was broken as the psychotic stowaway was shaken loose and he gasped as the truck came to a standstill, upside down a few yards from the road.

His head spinning, Howard unbuckled the seatbelt and tumbled loose, cutting himself in several places as he tried to scramble out of the wreckage of his truck. Once free, he stood up and looked about. He was some distance from the road and the woods loomed on his left. Behind him, pale in the moonlight, the figure who had tried to choke him was shambling towards him, a gangly, hideous thing with barely anything about its face that suggested a living human being.

Unable to comprehend what horror this was, Howard turned and ran towards the trees. He was miles from anywhere and there might not be any cars coming down the road until it was too late. This *thing*, whatever it was, wanted to kill him and, in his panicked mind, he knew that his only hope was to lose it in the woods.

He ran as fast as he could which was difficult due to the alcohol in his system and the tangled bushes and branches that clawed at him. It was a stumbling, frantic escape with no real direction in mind other than away from that thing that was pursuing him.

A glance over his shoulder made him nearly weep with terror as he saw the gangly, shriveled creature hacking its way through the undergrowth towards him, the moonlight glinting off a long piece of twisted metal he had torn from the smashed pickup.

Howard cried out as his foot caught on a root and he stumbled headlong. He scrabbled in the dirt as he tried to regain his feet, but he was too slow. The sharp rod of metal plunged down into his ankle, snapping his Achilles tendon as it passed through the flesh.

He screamed and then screamed again as the creature ripped the implement free and brought it up for another stab. Rolling to one side, Howard evaded the savage thrust of metal which embedded itself in the earth. He brought his injured leg up and tried to put some weight on it. It buckled under him, and, as he stumbled, he inadvertently ducked a swipe of the metal rod, its end red with his own blood. While the attacker was off balance, he got up and limped away, knowing that he was done for. He couldn't outrun this maniac now.

Sobbing as he pushed on through the bushes, he could hear the creature behind him, getting closer and closer. He fell against a tree trunk and gasped as the metal rod passed through his abdomen, skewering his innards. All the breath seemed sucked from him as sharp pain erupted in his chest. The end of the metal protruded from his ribcage like a toothpick in a sausage. Then it was sucked back out of him, dragging some of his guts with it.

He sank to his knees and slumped onto his back, wide eyes and blood-foaming mouth gawping up at his murderer. The man wasn't even alive! That was his last thought as the thing with the rotten face held the bloodied metal rod above his own face, droplets of gore dripping down onto him. *He isn't even alive.*

And then, neither was Howard as the metal slammed down into his eye socket, bursting the left half of his brain out through the back of his skull and shoving it deep down into the earth.

The Lipstadts had one of those irritatingly chirpy musical doorbells that rang to the tune of 'Oh, My Darling Clementine'. Mrs. Lipstadt thought it was cute but to Lauren it felt hideously tacky.

"I'll get it," said Harriet as she bounded from the kitchen, her hand shoved into a box of Cinnamon Toast Crunch.

Probably her boyfriend, Mike, Lauren thought with a touch of jealousy as she lounged on the sofa, half watching an episode of *21 Jump Street*.

Harriet fumbled with the chain that was always on the door now, even in the daytime. There'd been another murder last night. Some guy had been butchered up on the highway as it led into town. Some of the kids at school were saying that it was Toby Johnson's stepdad. Even though they always did their best to avoid each other, Lauren couldn't help feeling sorry for the odd kid with the black hair and heavy metal t-shirts. With his real dad murdered by Anthony Stevens and now his stepdad? How much bad luck could one kid take?

There was the sound of a woman's voice at the front door. Lauren could only catch a few words of the conversation before Harriet said; "Oh, I'm not Lauren, I'm Harriet. Wait just a second."

Lauren sat up.

"Hey, Lauren?" said Harriet, poking her head around the doorway to the living room. "Someone's here to see you."

Harriet disappeared back into the kitchen, still munching from the cereal box, leaving the front door open. Lauren got up and went out into the hallway.

A middle-aged woman was standing on the doorstep, dressed in smart business clothes. A Mercedes was parked on the street behind her.

"Hi, are you Lauren?" the woman said.

"Yes?" Lauren replied.

The woman extended her hand. "Agnes Goodman. I'm the daughter of Mrs. Wallace on the end of the street."

"Oh!" Lauren hadn't meant to sound so surprised but, in truth, she was. It was the first time she had seen any of the old woman's relatives.

"My mother seems to think that you helped her the other night, is that correct?"

"Well, it wasn't anything really," Lauren replied. "We found her wandering in her back garden, that is, the kid next door and me, and it was late and getting cold, so I just helped her back indoors. She seemed a bit confused ..."

"It's her medication," the woman replied, shaking her head. "She keeps forgetting to take it. I mean, what use is medication for Alzheimer's when they forget to take the damn stuff, right?" she affected an embarrassed smile. "I just came by to thank you for what you did."

"Oh, it was nothing, really."

"I know she belongs in a home, but she just won't go for it and I'm afraid it will take something really bad to happen before we can get her into one. We have help that stops by a couple of times a week to bring her groceries and make sure she takes her pills but it's not enough. I live in L.A. so I can't be out here every day. It's a great reassurance for us to know that she has such wonderful neighbors who'll look out for her."

"Um ..."

"That's all I wanted to say, really. And to apologize. Mother can get quite erratic when she doesn't take her meds. I hope she didn't scare you."

"Not at all," Lauren lied. "She wasn't making much sense, really."

"She never does when she has one of her episodes. I wouldn't pay her much attention. Well, I'd better be getting to my hotel. I'll be by in the morning to check up on Mother and then I'm heading back to L.A. It was nice to meet you, Lauren. And thank you once again."

"It was nice to meet you too," Lauren mumbled as Mrs. Goodman turned and headed to her car. As she closed the door, Lauren couldn't help but think that a woman who obviously had a good job in L.A. and enough money for a Mercedes, might be able to afford full-time care for her senile mother.

Toby met the others at the greasy pizza parlor in town the night after his stepdad's body was found butchered in the woods not far from his smashed-up pickup. Sheriff Weiss had come round to the house with the news and his mom had gone into hysterics while Toby and his little sister looked on, dumbly. Both of them knew that in one night, their world had changed for the better. Their mom would come to her senses eventually. She could finally start living the life she deserved, free from that abusive asshole.

But Toby guessed that Howard's death, not to mention the nature of it, brought back too many bad memories about his father's murder five years previously and he felt bad for that. And of course, there was the notion around town that it was the same guy who had killed both of them. Being one of only four people who knew that it was the truth – in a certain manner of speaking – made Toby want to laugh out loud.

The sheriff, of course, didn't put much stock in the theory and had told Mrs. Johnson so. "Ain't no way it was Anthony Stevens," he said in answer to her howls that the killer had it in for her family. "I put that mad dog down myself back in 'eighty-two. Just because his body was never found, doesn't mean he's still running around after all these years. This is the work of some new nut and poor Howard ran afoul of him through bad luck."

Right, thought Toby. *Poor Howard*. Like Sheriff Weiss didn't know what a piece of shit he was. He had even ignored the fading bruise around Toby's eye. Just like he ignored everything else. There had been a time when Toby had thought he might end up with Sheriff Weiss as a stepfather. He used to come around often enough to check up on Mom which was natural enough considering they had both lost their spouses that bad night back in 'eighty-two and that his father had been the sheriff's deputy. Toby guessed Sherrif Weiss also felt guilty for placing Toby's dad on watch in a car outside his house that night. Young Deputy Johnson had been the first to get it when Stevens had come looking for his daughter. Mrs. Weiss had been the next.

But any hopes Sheriff Weiss might have had of hooking up with the widow of the man he had gotten killed were dashed when she started dating Howard. Now he was out of the way, perhaps the sheriff would try his luck again, after letting her grieve a little, of course. That didn't bother Toby much. Hell, after Howard, anybody would be an improvement in the stepdad department. And if Sheriff Weiss started getting a tad too heavy handed in his treatment of his stepson, well, he might just get what his predecessor did.

The fact that the weird notebook Gary had procured was the real deal and, what was more, that Toby could actually make the spells work, had given him a confidence and sense of power that had been missing for most of his life. He had fucking done it! The other three had worried that the resurrection of Anthony Stevens had been a mistake due to Toby not understanding the ritual and, if he was totally honest, they were right. But the second ritual, in which he had commanded Stevens to kill his stepdad, had gone off without a hitch.

They had simply walked away from Stevens that night, leaving him in the gloom of the park, hoping to God that he wouldn't follow them to their homes. He had watched them leave, standing there, stock still like an abandoned puppy. They had gone back the next day, half expecting him to still be there but fortunately, he had wandered off to whatever part of the woods he called home, apparently awaiting their orders.

As before, it had fallen to Toby to do the ritual but this time he had done it in the privacy of his own bedroom, on his homemade altar to Satan. The ritual, as written in the book, required a personal object belonging to the would-be victim. That had been easy. Howard left his crap all over the house. He had taken a buck knife Howard kept on his nightstand and performed the ritual on it just as the book said to. The next night, Howard had been killed.

It was all too easy. He held the power of life and death in his hand. The others would have to respect him now. Todd could suck it. Brooke would soon come around to the idea of dating him instead of that jerk and there wasn't a damn thing Todd could do about it if he didn't want to end up like old Howard.

These were the thoughts that occupied Toby's giddy mind as he pushed open the door of the pizza parlor and met the others. Todd was shoving some kid away from the Double Dragon machine. It was that Corey Lutz kid who was always hanging around without any friends. Todd pushed him into a booth with the threat of a pounding and took over the game, dropping in a quarter and starting to pound the buttons instead. Brooke and Gary were sitting in a nearby booth looking pasty and nervous as they nursed their cokes. Toby slid in opposite them, and they looked at him expectantly, as if hoping that he would say something first.

"Dude," said Gary at last. "Your stepdad, man ..."

"Yeah, I know," he replied. Then he smiled. That shocked them. "Hey, what do you expect? Me to grieve for the bastard?"

"No," said Brooke, "but ... I mean ... *it worked.*"

"Fuck!" Todd yelled as his fighter took one too many hits from a street thug and died. He gave the arcade machine a violent shove and then came over to the booth, sliding in next to Brooke and looping his arm over her. "Damn right it worked!" he said. "I hear our boy messed up your old man pretty fucking hard!"

"Keep your voice down, idiot!" Gary hissed. "You wanna tell the whole world about what we did?"

"Relax," said Todd with a dismissive wave of his hand. "No one's listening. Anyway, nobody can prove anything 'cause it wasn't us! That's the beauty of it. We weren't even there. Now, about our next victim. I got the perfect subject. That dried up old bitch, Mrs. Ross."

"Hold up!" said Gary, barely able to keep his own voice down now. "You wanna kill a fucking teacher?"

"Are they an endangered species or something?" Todd fired back. "That bitch is gonna make me fail physics and then I'll be busting my ass in my dad's factory for the rest of my life. And my dad is an asshole of a boss. He won't go easy on me."

"You didn't make the sacrifice," said Toby, glaring at him.

"What did you say?"

"I said, you didn't make the sacrifice. You don't have any control over ... *him*."

"Then you can do it for me, Johnson," Todd said dangerously. "What fucking difference does it make to you? Do the magic ritual like you did for your stepdad."

"This isn't a game, Todd," said Toby. "This is murder."

"Oh, you think I'm fucking playing around?" Todd was yelling now and standing up in the booth, towering over Toby.

"Calm down!" Brooke said, hauling on her boyfriend's shoulder. "Jeez. Gary's right, we need to be careful what we say."

Gary glanced nervously around the pizza parlor. There was nobody at the counter and Corey Lutz had reclaimed the Double Dragon machine and was entirely engrossed in beating up tough guys. There was one couple over in the booth near the door who were looking at them suspiciously. "Yeah," he said. "Keep it down or take it outside, Todd."

"I will fucking take it outside if this little freak keeps giving me hassle," Todd seethed as he sat back down.

"I don't think we should do this again," said Brooke. "It's too dangerous."

"Yeah, Brooke's right," Gary agreed. "People are gonna get suspicious if we keep doing it. I mean, what are the chances that everybody we don't like keeps getting offed?"

"Oh, so Johnson here gets to kill his stepdad but when I want a turn, you guys lose your nerve? Some friends!"

"Let's just stop talking about it," said Gary. "I'm hungry."

They ordered pizza and ate in silence. Toby kept glancing at Todd with his arm around Brooke as he stuffed pizza into his fat face, eating with his mouth open like a pig. Now that his stepdad was gone, Toby didn't think there was anybody else in the world he hated more than Todd Cates.

CHAPTER 8

That Friday, Lauren sat with her back against the sticker-encrusted dresser in Corey's attic bedroom which was an Aladdin's cave of boyhood curiosity. Posters of planets and galaxies plastered the slanted ceiling from which model UFOs and space shuttles dangled on wires and every shelf and surface was cluttered with comic books, disassembled electronics, *Return of the Jedi* toys, science kit paraphernalia and books on the 'uneXplained' and the 'X-traordinary' and other things where the letter 'X' took prominence.

Corey was lying on his bed in his PJs and idly leafing through an Iron Man comic book. Lauren was holding one of Corey's walkie talkies and, flipping the on switch, held it up to her mouth. "Earth calling Corey, Earth calling Corey, time for bed!"

Corey grinned and held his own up and answered; "Negative, negative! The Serpent Squad remain undefeated!"

He'd had Lauren hiding all around the house in an elaborate game of hide and seek with the walkie talkies for most of the evening. Now she was looking forward to getting him off to sleep so she could watch a movie downstairs in peace.

"Do you think Mrs. Wallace has been contacted by aliens, and that's why she's so weird?" Corey asked her. "I saw this program once about this guy who had been abducted and they took a part of his brain and he acted really weird afterwards."

"Mrs. Wallace isn't weird," Lauren said. "She's senile. Her daughter came round the other day to thank me on her behalf. She heard that I helped her indoors and I guess she just wanted to explain. Her mother sometimes forgets to take her medication and that can

73

make her confused. That's why she was acting so strange."

"Still pretty weird if you ask me. Maybe her daughter's an alien. Or a government agent sent to cover things up. Makes sense. *I've* never seen her daughter before. In fact, nobody has."

"Come on, you, it's time you got into bed."

"Lauren?" Corey asked as he tossed the comic book onto his cluttered nightstand.

"Yeah?"

"Who do you think murdered those campers and that other guy on the highway?"

Lauren glanced at him. "I don't know, Corey. But Sheriff Weiss seems to think it's some crazy person from out of town."

"Then you don't think it was ..."

"My father?"

He nodded.

She shook her head. "Don't listen to what the kids say at school. Everybody seems to think he's come back but he hasn't."

"Not me."

"Good. Anthony Stevens is dead. Sheriff Weiss shot him years ago."

"Lauren?"

She sighed. "Yes?"

"I don't know who the murderer is, but I think some of the kids in your school might be involved."

"Oh? And what wild conspiracy theory is this now?"

"It's not a conspiracy theory! I overheard them talking in the pizza parlor. I was playing Double Dragon and they thought I wasn't listening, but I was."

"Who?"

"Brooke McKenna and her boyfriend and those other two who always hang out with them."

"Valerie and Jackie?

"No, two guys. One wears makeup and has his hair dyed black. Looks like a devil worshipper. I think it was his stepdad who got murdered."

"Oh. You mean Toby and Gary. What were they saying?"

"Really crazy stuff. The way they talked about the Satan guy's stepdad made it seem like they killed him or at least had him killed by somebody else. They kept talking about sacrifice and a ritual and who their next target was gonna be. I think Todd said something about a Mrs. Ross?"

"She's our physics teacher," said Lauren. "Todd hates her. They were probably just fantasizing. Talking big. I wouldn't worry about it."

"One of them – not the Satan guy – kept telling them to keep it down, like he was scared of being overheard. Then Todd got mad because they had let the Satan guy kill his stepdad and now they weren't letting him have his turn. Brooke had to calm him down, like she didn't want a scene."

"That's a first for her," Lauren said, bitterly.

"You don't like Brooke very much, do you?"

"No, I don't. Look, I'm sure it was all just loudmouthing and make-believe. It's better if you stay away from those guys, huh? They're bad news."

"No kidding. Especially that Todd guy. He's a major dweeb."

"All right, tough guy. Sleep time."

He scrambled under the covers and Lauren tucked him in before heading over to the door and flipping off the light switch.

"Hey, Lauren?" he asked, as she was about to leave.

"Yeah?"

"Could you leave the light on the landing on? And my door open just a little?"

She smiled. "Sure."

The bell rang, signaling the end of classes for the day and Toby grabbed his stuff from his locker, shoving books into his black backpack with the inverted pentagram patch on it. Slinging it over his shoulder, he headed for the exit. As he was walking along the side of the brick bike sheds, Todd caught up to him and drew him to one side.

"Look man, you gotta help me with that problem I spoke to you about," he said in what he probably considered a conspiratorial whisper. "The bitch is really on my case about me cutting class last week and I want her finished! She's threatening to send a letter home. My dad's gonna beat my ass, man."

"That's rough," Toby said, not the least bit interested in Todd's problems.

"So, how about tonight?" Todd asked hopefully. "We do the ritual, *our buddy* does his thing and no more hassle for me, right?"

"I thought we'd agreed to leave it," Toby said. "Gary's pretty freaked. He might blab."

"Hey, *I'll* handle Gary, don't worry about that."

"Well, I still think we should just drop it. I mean, it's a teacher, y'know? Things could get pretty hot for us ..."

Todd's friendly demeanor turned suddenly vicious, and he grabbed Toby by his denim jacket and dragged him behind the bike shed, slamming him up against the brick wall. The back of Toby's head smacked the brickwork and he saw stars.

"Listen, you make-up wearing queer, I'm serious!" Todd snarled. "If you don't play ball then I'll make sure everybody knows that it was you who killed your stepdad. I'll say you are into some spooky occult shit and that you hexed him or whatever. You think we're all in this together? You're wrong! I'll say the rest of us had no idea what you were doing. Who do you think everybody will believe? Some normal teenagers or the freaky satanist who has a fucking pentagram on his backpack?"

Toby squirmed in Todd's grip, but it was no use. Todd was a big guy and had him pinned. He could smell his bad breath and feel the heat of his rage and, for a moment, he felt like he did whenever Howard had picked on him. It was a feeling he swore he would never feel again and his hatred for Todd reached new heights.

"OK!" he said through gritted teeth.

"OK what?"

"OK, I'll help you. I don't give a shit, just let me go!"

Todd released him and gave him a shove for good measure. "Tonight. Where shall we do it?"

"I need to get the book from my house ..."

"Then we'll do it at your house. See you in one hour?"

"Well, my mom is working tonight so ... I guess ..."

"Perfect!"

He sauntered off and Toby picked up his backpack, rubbed the back of his head and headed for home, swearing vengeance on Todd Cates.

They came over before his mom left for work, or at least, Brooke and Todd did. Gary was a no-show. Toby's mom seemed surprised that he had 'friends' over. He guessed he never really had, at least not since elementary school.

"Look, no big parties tonight, OK?" she said to him in the kitchen before she left. "I think it's great that you're making more friends but, just no parties, huh? Not with everything that's happened. Remember that your sister is here."

"Sure, Mom. We're just gonna hang out."

77

She blew him a kiss and left.

His sister was watching TV in the living room and ignored the trio as they headed up to Toby's bedroom. Toby's head swam as the reality of Brooke being in his bedroom hit him. It was practically enough to give him a boner. She looked around at his heavy metal posters and satanic paraphernalia with cautious curiosity bordering on alarm.

"Where's Gary?" Toby asked, trying to pay it cool.

"That fucker's pussying out," Todd said as he peered around at Toby's morbid décor with distaste. Toby had spraypainted a lot of plastic skulls black and strung them up with inverted crosses above his altar. "Jesus, it looks like Halloween in here."

"Do you think he'll tell anybody?"

"Not if he knows what's good for him. Right, shall we get down to business? I don't want to spend a second more in this mausoleum than I have to."

"Make yourselves comfortable," Toby said and when Brooke sat down on his bed, he found his neck burning crimson. "Uh, I have like, an altar over here. We can do the ritual on that."

"An altar?" Todd said. "Jesus, Johnson, you really take this shit seriously."

"Shouldn't we all?" Brooke said. "I mean, it works. We really brought back the dead."

"Sure, I guess. Whatever helps, Johnson. I just want that bitch Mrs. Ross to get what's coming to her."

"Did you bring something that belongs to her?" Toby asked. "You remember that that's part of the ritual?"

"You think I'm a dumbass? Of course I did. Here." He pulled a tube of lipstick from his jeans pocket. "I swiped it from her desk today."

"OK, whatever," said Toby, taking the lipstick and placing it on the altar. "Now I need the book."

He realized with a sudden panic that the book was in the drawer of his nightstand. *Along with the polaroid of Brooke*. If either Brooke or her dumb boyfriend saw that picture, his life would be over. He opened the drawer just wide enough to slip his hand in to retrieve the book. As he removed it, he caught a glimpse of Brooke's face in the bottom of the drawer, the real-life version only a few feet away, totally oblivious as was her boyfriend. *How little you know, Todd, you fucking prick!*

He lit a candle on the altar and opened the book on the right page. Beneath the resurrection ritual, was the spell for cursing somebody using a 'revenant'. The book didn't explicitly state it, but as far as Toby was concerned, the revenant in question could be none other than the spirit brought back by the ritual a few pages earlier. At least, that was how it seemed to work.

"By the powers of His Satanic Majesty!" he began. "Mighty Master of Evil and most respected foe of Jehovah and all his angels! I call to you, my servant, whose body I have summoned from beyond the veil of death. I call upon you to do this service in the name of Satan! See this object I place before you. Destroy, crush, strangle, kill *Audrey Ross*, the owner of this object. May she dilute, languish, sink and may all her limbs dissolve! My servant, I call upon you to complete this task."

He closed the book and blew out the candle. As he picked up the lipstick, he thought he could feel the latent power vibrating from the small object. It was cursed now and would bring the specter of death upon its owner.

He handed it to Todd. "Make sure you put this back in Mrs. Ross's desk," he told him. "It won't work if it is no longer in her possession."

"Will do," said Todd, wide eyed as he accepted the object. Apparently, he could feel its power too or maybe he was just gleeful at the vengeance that was soon to be visited on his nemesis.

"Come on, Todd," said Brooke, getting up off the bed. "Let's go."

"You can just stay and ... hang out?" Toby said, hating how he made it sound like a question.

"No fucking thank you," said Todd, giving Toby's room a final scathing look. "The local cemetery is more cheerful. Come on, babe, let's hit the mall and grab some fries."

Brooke followed him out and neither saw the dark look cross Toby's face. *Just you wait, Todd,* he thought to himself. *You won't be such a comedian when I'm done with you. And Brooke will be mine!*

CHAPTER 9

Bored with the Tuesday night movie, Mrs. Ross aimed the remote at the TV set and flipped the channel to catch the last half of *Moonlighting* with Bruce Willis and Cybill Shepherd. As if in protest, her dog, Dougie, a small Yorkshire Terrier, jumped down off the couch and ran over to the sliding doors that looked out into the garden. It began to bark angrily and jump up, putting its front paws on the glass.

"Hush down, Dougie!" Mrs. Ross chided him. "I can't hear the TV!"

Dougie ignored her, alternating between barking and whining. Mrs. Ross sighed and got up. "All right, all right, I'm coming."

She went over to the window and looked out. Her immaculate garden was shrouded in gloom, and she couldn't see anything that the little dog might be so excited about. He continued to whine and looked up at her expectantly.

"You need to go pee? It can't wait until our nine o'clock walk?" she asked him.

He stared at her with big, brown eyes. She unlatched the door and slid it open just enough so the little dog could slip through.

As soon as it was open, the dog bolted and streaked across the lawn to vanish into the darkness.

"Hey!" Mrs. Ross cried. "Where are you running off to?"

She slid the door open wider and stepped out onto her patio. The evening air was chill, and cut through her gray sweatsuit. She hugged her arms against the cold and yelled Dougie's name. There was no sound but the rustling of the wind in the trees.

Dougie, you little shit, she thought as she ventured into the garden. She had no desire to be wandering about outside after dark. Not when there was a killer on the loose. The murders had taken place up on Mount Lenzi and not down in the suburbs, but still, it was a morbid thought and she wanted to be safely behind locked doors, not rummaging around in the bushes for her dog.

"Dougie!" she yelled, angry now. What had gotten into him? She was tired from work and wanted to relax in front of the box. Where the hell had he got to?

There was a loose plank in the backyard fence that Dougie liked to squeeze through to get into her neighbor's garden. She had been planning to fix it for weeks now but never remembered to. Squatting down, she peered through the gap in the wood and could see Dougie scampering about next door.

"Dougie, you get back here!" she snapped. "Right now!"

The dog was freaked about something and was sniffing around like crazy. She yelled at him again, really losing her temper now, and he reluctantly headed over to her. Reaching her hand through the gap in the fence, she grabbed him by his collar and dragged him into her arms.

"Now, what was all that about?" she said to him as she carried him back to the house. "Making me go ferreting about in the bushes for you after dark!"

As she approached the sliding door to her house, a horrible feeling crept over her. She had left it wide open. Sure, she hadn't been gone long, but long enough for somebody to slip in while her back was turned. It wasn't very likely that somebody had got in, but the possibility was there, and it made her acutely nervous.

Somebody *could* have been waiting in her backyard for her to open the door and then snuck in as soon as she had stepped out. They *could* have concealed themselves in the shadows over by the potting shed there. They *could* have planned it in advance.

She was being silly, she knew. It was the lateness of the hour and the gruesome murders up in the hills that had her spooked. But then, what had got Dougie all riled up in the first place?

Stupid! Stupid! She chided herself as she went indoors and slid the door shut behind her, locking it.

She set Dougie down and he scampered off towards his basket. Her nerves were still jangling, and she desperately wanted a smoke. She was trying to give them up but still had a pack in her purse for emergencies. She wasn't going cold turkey, just trying to cut down.

She fetched her purse from the table by the front door and rummaged around in it for her cigarettes and lighter. Her fingers closed around her tube of red lipstick that she hadn't been able to find earlier today. That was weird. She always kept it in her desk drawer in her classroom. Had she put it in here by mistake? No wonder she hadn't been able to find it.

Shaking her head at how scatty she was being, she lit a cigarette and sucked the smoke into her lungs, letting the nicotine calm her nerves. But the bad thing about smoking was that it always made her want a drink.

She wasn't much of a midweek drinker but living alone occasionally got her spooked and even with Dougie for company, she sometimes felt very vulnerable. She went into the kitchen and opened the cupboard above the sink. Reaching in between the cereal boxes, she retrieved her bottle of vodka. She placed it on the kitchen counter and then opened the refrigerator for orange juice to mix up a screwdriver.

As she closed the refrigerator door, she uttered a cry and the carton of juice tumbled to the floor, orange liquid sweeping across the linoleum. The lit cigarette tumbled from her lips to land in it with a sizzle. In the doorway to the living room stood a man, filthy and ragged looking. His face was a mask of rotten flesh and she hoped to God that it really was just a mask.

"Who ... who are you?" she stammered.

The figure didn't answer her. He had clearly snuck in while the patio door had been open and had been watching her for the last few minutes. Her worst fears had come true.

With a sudden movement, the man lunged for her, bony hands reaching outward. She turned and tried to flee but slipped on the spilled orange juice and landed heavily on the kitchen floor with a cry as pain lanced through her hip.

The man was almost on top of her but crashed into the open refrigerator door, making the bottles and jars in it rattle, giving her a couple of seconds to scramble to her feet and bolt for the front door.

Dougie had rocketed from his basket, barking frantically as the man got up and chased Mrs. Ross out into the hall. She had just been able to open the front door before the palm of his hand slammed against it, shutting it again. His other hand went for her throat but Dougie, Lord bless that dog, had fastened his teeth into the man's ankle and was doing his damndest to tear a chunk out of his leg.

The man showed no sign of pain but looked down at the resilient dog in irritation. With a savage jerk of his leg, he sent the dog cartwheeling across the kitchen. The distraction had provided Mrs. Ross with the opportunity to run for the stairs but the maniac was fast on her heels, grabbing one leg by the calf, fingers digging in deep, and pulling her back down.

Mrs. Ross screamed as her chin hit the carpeted stairs and she tumbled down on her front, barreling into the intruder. Dougie was still making a racket and dancing around the man as he got up and grabbed Mrs. Ross around the throat.

She tried to scream but her slowly constricting windpipe wouldn't let out anything more than a harsh whistle. She held onto the intruder's forearms, trying to force them apart but couldn't. His foul stench seeped into her nostrils and did as good a job at choking her as the hard thumbs which were pressing into her throat.

He squeezed harder and those bony digits penetrated flesh. Mrs. Ross jerked spasmodically, pain lancing through her body. She could feel his thumbs inside her throat as her lungs choked on blood. She convulsed, blood bursting up through the hole in her neck, passing around the man's thumbs and running down the front of her sweatshirt.

Still, the man continued to squeeze. He kept on squeezing until he felt bone crack and cartilage crunch under his hands. Then, he released his victim and she fell back against the stairs, her head striking the bottom step and resting at an awkward angle. Blood still pumped out of her ruined throat and soaked into the carpet.

The killer took a second to admire his handiwork, and then walked back through the kitchen, ignoring the frantic yapping of the dog, as he made his way out the patio door and into the darkness of the back yard from where he had come.

The students in the school auditorium listened in somber, numbed silence as Principal Jevicky addressed them. The teachers lined the walls on both sides of the stage, looking like they'd all been punched in the gut. Some were teary-eyed. Everybody had been pulled in for this impromptu address in their first period. For some, it had come out of the blue. They had thought it was going to be another dressing down about satanic graffiti behind the bike sheds, but most had heard the news over breakfast. News, especially bad news, travelled fast in a town as small as Crimson Bay.

"Now, I'm sure you're all as deeply upset as I am about the tragic loss of Mrs. Ross," Principal Jevicky said. "But I ask that you all remain strong and carry on as normal. The school nurse will be here every day in case any of you want to ... um, *talk* to her."

There were some eyerolls and stifled grins in the audience as Principal Jevicky started to flounder a little. He was great at laying down the law but when it came to sensitivity, he was all at sea. "Mr. Bowman will be taking physics classes for the foreseeable future," he went on, "until an adequate, um, replacement for Mrs. Ross can be found. Now, I have asked Sheriff Weiss to come down here today to talk to you all about safety precautions during these ... ah, difficult times. Sheriff?"

Sheriff Weiss took to the podium. "Good morning, kids," he said. "I'm sorry about the dreadful news you've all received this morning, but I want to assure you all that the sheriff's department is doing everything it can to catch the perpetrator of these awful murders."

Jeff Duvall raised his hand. "Is it Anthony Stevens, Sheriff?"

The question caused a hubbub of excitement and the teachers tried to calm everybody down. Lauren's neck and cheeks burned red as she felt the eyes of several students on her and she sank down in her chair, wishing that she could just vanish.

"Now, I want to make one thing clear to you kids," said Sheriff Weiss, raising his hands for quiet, a fresh sternness in his voice. "We have no reason whatsoever to believe that Anthony Stevens has returned or is even alive. Please refrain from spreading rumors."

"Then who is it, Sheriff?" another kid asked.

"We're unable to give you any information on that at this time," Sheriff Weiss said. "But I will be having a meeting with your folks at the town hall this evening to inform them about some safety measures. I feel that it is only fair that I tell you kids right now that there is going to be a curfew from seven p.m. to six a.m. effective as of this evening."

There was an outburst of groans at this.

"All we're trying to do is keep you all safe," Sheriff Weiss said apologetically. "This killer, whoever he is, preys on victims at night. You kids have no business being out after dark in any case."

Lauren heard somebody behind her mumble; "Wasn't Mrs. Ross killed inside her own house?"

After they were dismissed and sent off to their classes, Lauren spotted Brooke and Todd talking to Gary and Toby. Their conversation seemed to get a little heated and Gary suddenly threw up his arms and stormed off. Todd looked like he was going to chase after him, but Brooke pulled on his arm to keep him from doing so.

What the hell was that all about? Lauren felt a chill as she remembered what Corey had told her. He had overheard them talking about killing Mrs. Ross. About using magic rituals and sacrifices. She could well believe that Toby would attempt that sort of thing – everybody knew he was into the occult – but had he convinced the others to take part? And had it actually worked?

She tried to stop herself thinking like that. Of course black magic and satanic rituals didn't work. They *couldn't* have killed Mrs. Ross. But the coincidence was certainly eerie.

Corey wasn't to be dissuaded. "*Now* do you believe me?" he said, as she walked up the yard to the Lipstadt's house after school that day. It seemed like he had been waiting in the front garden for her and she wouldn't have put it past him. "Those guys were talking about killing Mrs. Ross and a few days later she ends up dead. There's *no way* you can put that down as a coincidence."

"And there's *no way* you can convince me that they're using black magic to put spells on people," she told him. "Mrs. Ross was murdered by some sicko, not those losers. Sheriff Weiss told us not to spread false rumors, so you'd better let it drop."

"First Amendment rights, man!" said Corey.

"Right on, brother!" she said, flashing him the peace sign. "See you on Friday. We're burdened with each other again, I'm afraid."

Corey shrugged. "Fine by me. Can you bring popcorn again?"

"Sure."

On Thursday evening, Lauren was helping with the planning of the drama club's production of *A Midsummer Night's Dream*. It was only in the early stages of planning and wouldn't be shown until the end of the school year, but Mr. Hinzman, the drama teacher, wanted to get off to an early start after last year's fiasco in which the paint on the sets were barely dry and hardly anybody had learned their lines.

Lauren had once been an active member of the drama club with dreams of being an actress but, since the murders five years ago, had found herself shrinking from the spotlight. She was happy to help out with the behind-the-scenes stuff like set design, but the thought of standing on stage in front of a bunch of people who hated her and would most likely boo and throw things at her filled her with dread.

Mr. Hinzman had sent her down into the school basement to find the roll of cloth that had bricks painted on which could serve as Tom Snout's wall in the play-within-a-play. The cloth had been a backdrop in a previous production of *West Side Story* and, with the budget being what it was, Mr. Hinzman was all about recycling.

The school basement was not how Lauren had wanted to spend her afternoon. Gloomy and full of oddities, it was a spooky place even in the middle of the day when the school was full of people. But now, after everybody had gone home, with the sky outside the small, high windows darkening with the onset of evening, it was positively eerie. Here were the relics of past decades, forgotten about for the most part. Old desks marked with graffiti by students who had long since graduated were piled on top of each other. The shadows cloaked shelves of boxes while dressmaker dolls lurked in the corners and cobwebs and dust lay thick on everything.

The drama stuff was kept in the dingiest part of the basement, far from the shifting light of the gently swaying lightbulb. Rolls of fabric had been shoved behind plywood constructions of cannibalized sets, racks of costumes and boxes of props. Lauren wrinkled her nose at the floating dust particles as she rummaged through the detritus, looking for the brick-painted cloth.

One box yielded a bunch of stuff that had nothing to do with drama and she figured had been placed here by mistake. It held things like broken sports trophies, old yearbooks and a bunch of framed photographs. She rifled through the photographs out of interest, glancing at the black and white faces of students and teachers who had long since moved on and then froze as she saw the face of Anthony Stevens, aged eighteen or nineteen, staring out of the pool of buzz-cuts, side partings, beehives and Alice bands of the class of 1968.

A chill rippled through her as she instantly recognized the face which had haunted her for the past five years. He had been significantly older and more weathered by fourteen years in prison when he had abducted her, but the papers had been filled with pictures of him from before his incarceration that she would recognize him anywhere.

The photograph had obviously been taken down from the wall of class photos in the hallway outside the principal's office and, in fact, Lauren had seen the bare patch of wall where it had hung and had never thought much about it. Clearly the school wasn't too keen to count a mass murderer among its alumni and somebody had taken the picture down and hidden it down here with all the other things to be forgotten about.

She gazed at the faces in the picture and spotted her mom and then her dad, or at least, the man she had called 'Dad' for most of her life. Ronette Shaye and Josh Mackenzie looked like model students; her mom pretty in a dress with blonde pigtails and her dad clearly a jock with the build of a linebacker and a severe flattop. She missed them dreadfully and her eyes kept being drawn back to the cold, emotionless stare of the boy who would one day murder them; Anthony Stevens, her *real* father.

He had been a reedy kid with a weirdly angular face and black, greasy hair which she had inherited. Despite all the things that she knew about him and all the awful crimes he had committed, it was hard to see such wickedness in the fresh-faced kid in the picture. He looked so young, but she knew that even at that age, he had already started abusing kids.

She shuddered and was about to shove the framed photograph down to the bottom of the box, when she spotted another face she recognized.

She hadn't thought to look at the teacher but now that she did, she saw a friendly-looking woman with a beehive and a floral print dress. She was twenty-odd years younger in the picture, but Lauren instantly knew who she was looking at, the list of names at the bottom of the photograph confirming it.

Mrs. Wallace.

The crazy old lady at the end of her street had been her parents' teacher? Why had nobody told her? The Lipstadts had moved to Crimson Bay after her parents had graduated so she guessed they hadn't known. But in all her years, nobody had ever mentioned that Mrs. Wallace had once been a teacher at Crimson Bay High.

She wondered when Mrs. Wallace's mind had gone and if something had caused it. She must have been approaching retirement in the photograph but to go from being a happy-looking high school teacher to the local weirdo who spoke to trees in the space of twenty years? She couldn't help but think the awfulness of Antony Stevens had played some part in it.

"Lauren?" a voice called from the stairs to the basement.

Lauren jumped and nearly dropped the photograph. "Yes, Mr. Hinzman?"

"Are you still down here? Did you find the bricks?"

"Uh, not yet."

"I'll come help you."

Lauren quickly shoved the photograph back in the box and replaced the lid.

CHAPTER 10

Sheriff Weiss parked outside his house and tried not to notice how dark and gloomy it looked compared to the other homes on the tree-lined street with their lit windows and flickering TV sets as families relaxed together for the evening. Since Martha had died and their daughter Chrissy had gone off to college, Sheriff Weiss tried to spend as little time as possible in the home they had made so pleasant with their presence. Work was his refuge now, but even he had to hit the sack once in a while and so he reluctantly drifted back to this empty shell of his former life each night to catch some zeds.

There seemed to be little point in going home for any other reason and he always stayed at the station house for as long as possible, finishing up paperwork and going over reports before Katie the fifty-two-year-old night dispatcher insisted that he headed home, chiding him like an exasperated mother. He usually returned to the station sometime the next morning wearing the creased shirt he had slept in and smelling faintly of whisky. Nobody said anything, not just because he was the boss, but because if anybody deserved to hit the bottle a little heavily, then it was Sheriff Weiss.

He hung his coat up and kicked off his shoes before heading into the living room, grabbing the half-empty bottle of scotch from the sideboard (where he had left it last night), and flipped the TV set on to Johnny Carson's *Tonight Show*. He unbuckled his belt and laid the holstered weight of his Smith and Wesson K-frame on the cluttered coffee table in front of him and flopped down on the couch, unscrewing the cap on the bottle.

Even as he drank whiskey from the bottle and watched Johnny Carson in his own living room, Sheriff Weiss couldn't help chewing over the case in his mind. There was no 'off switch' for a sheriff. Not when there was a killer to catch.

Could the murders have been committed by the same perp? That was the question he kept coming back to. The methods were entirely different. The campers and Howard DeAngelo had been stabbed while Audrey Ross had been strangled. Strangulation was almost always a crime of passion, though Sheriff Weiss had no idea who'd want to kill poor Audrey Ross. Her ex-husband was the only natural suspect, but he was confirmed to be in Las Vegas and had an alibi for the night of the crime.

When you looked at it, DeAngelo was the real anomaly. He had been skewered with a piece of his pickup's smashed bumper which was about as unpremeditated as you could get. And the campers had been stabbed to death with a kitchen knife from their own dinette, not a knife the killer had brought with him for the job. If the same guy had done all four murders, it was as if he was simply using whatever was to hand at the scene of the crime. Audrey Ross had been strangled because ... what? There were no knives in her kitchen?

That didn't make any sense. Sheriff Weiss had seen the knife block on her counter himself and her kitchen drawers contained all manner of things that could be used as a weapon. Instead, the killer had strangled her with enough force to drive his own thumbs through her windpipe. It was the ferocity that he found so unnerving.

That same ferocity could be seen in the way the two campers had been brutally, absolutely *brutally* stabbed to death. And DeAngelo? Hell, Sheriff Weiss didn't know what it took to make a guy shove a twisted piece

94

of bumper through somebody's eye socket, but he guessed it was beyond most people.

Perhaps it was the same perp after all and a completely unhinged one at that. The ferocity seemed to match, even if the methods didn't.

And that led him to ponder how premeditated any of the murders were. Generally, a murderer brought their own weapon to the party, unless it was a sudden, heat of the moment deal. And that kind of murderer usually didn't kill again. Grabbing whatever was to hand and using their own hands if there wasn't anything, was decidedly not how serial killers tended to operate.

A serial killer.

The more he thought about it, the less able he was to draw away from that horrifying conclusion. After all it had been through, Crimson Bay now had a serial killer. Just their fucking luck.

A copycat?

That was a possibility. After all, what were the chances that Crimson Bay would be visited by two entirely unconnected spree killers in less than ten years? The odds were astronomical. If they really did have a serial killer on their hands, then Sheriff Weiss would be willing to bet that they had been inspired by Anthony Stevens.

He sighed and took another swig from the bottle as Carson continued to do his schtick on TV. This damn job was like whack-a-mole, even when it came to murderers. He'd shot Anthony Stevens dead himself only for another sicko to rear his psycho head five years later. It was like the world enjoyed playing one big joke on the inhabitants of Crimson Bay and, he for one, was pig sick of it.

"Man, fuck this curfew!" Todd said to Brooke as they sat on the low wall near the school's entrance. "If they think they can keep us indoors then they've got another thing coming. You wanna grab some beers and ride around tonight?"

It was Friday afternoon, and the sun was shining through the orange leaves of the trees at the edge of the parking lot, giving everything a golden hue as the kids of Crimson Bay High filed out of the main building.

"My parents will try and keep me in ..." Brooke said. "It's like they've finally remembered I exist after five years."

"Fuck them! I'll come pick you up. You can sneak out your bedroom window, right?"

"I guess." Brooke had never needed to sneak out before. She had never been visible enough to her parents for them to stop her from going out but now, with all these killings, it was a different story. Her mom in particular seemed to be on the verge of a nervous breakdown about it all.

"Where the fuck is Gary?" she asked.

"I don't know, he's been acting real weird the last couple of days. I think he's totally lost his balls over the whole book thing. Offing old Mrs. Ross was the last straw. Me, I'm as happy as a pig in shit. We've got a substitute teacher who doesn't know his ass from his elbow and my grade will stay at a safe average. Misson accomplished."

"Here comes Toby. Man, he looks pissed."

"That's just how he looks, babe. It's part of his whole aesthetic."

But Toby *was* pissed, *really* pissed about something. He hurled his backpack at the wall they were sitting on in frustration and ran his hands through his black hair.

"Something up in spooksville, Johnson?" Todd asked.

"That fucking asshole Jevicky!" Toby snarled. "He took the book!"

Todd and Brooke sat bolt upright, their eyes wide. "You mean *the* book?" Todd asked.

"Yeah, *the* book. He confiscated it. Said it was inappropriate to have satanic garbage like that in school. He said the board takes a dim view on the occult."

"How the hell did you let him see it?" Todd snapped.

"Yeah," added Brooke, "and why the fuck did you bring it to school?"

"I never leave it anywhere," Toby said. "Not even in my room. My mom sometimes goes through my stuff looking for drugs. Jevicky stopped me as I was on my way out and made me empty out my bag. It's because of that graffiti behind the bike sheds. He's had me pegged for that ever since it happened. I guess he was hoping to find some spray cans in my backpack."

"Instead he found the fucking book?" Brooke said.

"Cool it, babe," said Todd, putting his meaty arm around her. "What's old Jevicky gonna make of it except satanic scribbles? Everybody knows Johnson here is into that shit. He probably won't even look through it. There's no way it can be tied to anything we've done. No way."

"Are you so sure?" Toby asked. "If anything gets out about how those people died, then old Jevicky might start taking a closer look at that book. And I don't like the way Gary has been acting lately."

"You think he might rat?"

"He might if he thinks he can get himself off the hook by dumping us all in it. That book in Jevicky's possession is like a time bomb. We need to get it back so there is nothing, and I mean *nothing*, to connect us to the murders."

"Well, what do you suggest?" asked Todd. "Bust into the school tonight and grab it back?"

"Pretty much," said Toby. "Only, not exactly *bust* in. Not when Gary has a key to the sports hall."

"He still has that?" Brooke asked.

"Yeah," said Todd. "It was his mom's and I guess nobody thought to ask for it back. We've sometimes talked about having an all-night party at the school but never got around to it. Guess tonight's the big night!"

"And it's a way to bring Gary back into line," said Toby. "If he helps us get that book back, then he's as guilty as the rest of us. He won't be able to drop us in the shit and cut a deal with the cops."

"Good plan," said Todd. "But where is he?"

"I saw him slip out the side entrance," Toby said. "Avoiding us as usual."

Todd slipped down off the wall and pounded his fist into his palm. "Then let's catch up with old Gary and have a little talk!"

Lauren had seen Gary sneak out the school's side entrance and had considered following him but decided that tailing the other three might be more profitable, if considerably more dangerous. She had been keeping a close eye on the gang ever since Mrs. Ross's death. She couldn't help it. It wasn't that she truly believed they were behind the murders, but there were just too many coincidences for her mind to let it rest until she had disproved Corey's outlandish theory conclusively.

There were clearly problems in the group. Gary had been purposely avoiding the other three all week after whatever that argument had been about on Tuesday. Now he was trying to slip away after school without running into the others. Brooke and Todd left with

Todd's arm over Brooke, and Lauren stalled for a few minutes at her locker while Toby walked past. She followed him out and saw him meet up with Brooke and Todd at the school entrance.

She kept her distance, not wanting to draw any attention to herself and, from across the grassy verge, was unable to hear anything Toby said to the others. He seemed to be venting about Principal Jevicky and then, with apparently great determination about something, the trio cut across the parking lot and headed around the side of the school.

The eastern side of the school faced a gradual slope of trees and paths that led down to the affluent suburbs of Crimson Bay. A few students made their way home down those dirt paths, but they were few and far between and it was a peaceful spot with the late afternoon sun streaming through the silent pines.

Lauren knew she was playing with fire by following the trio of troublemakers, but she knew that something was going on with them and she needed to know what. Hanging back as much as she could to keep out of sight, she caught up with them just as they caught up with Gary.

She halted as their voices reached her through the trees. Todd was giving Gary a hard time and she could see him pushing the skinny kid up against a tree.

"You're not thinking of ratting on us are you, Gary?" Todd snarled.

"N ... No!" Gary spluttered. "I swear!"

"Good. Because we're in this together and if one of us goes down, then we all do, got it?"

"Yeah! Come on, man, lemme go!"

But Todd didn't let hm go. "Why have you been avoiding us?" Brooke asked.

"I thought it was best we weren't seen together after ... *you know.*"

"Yeah, well it looks a whole lot more suspicious that you keep running away from us."

"All right, whatever, man, just let me go!"

Todd released him and he backed away, rearranging his t-shirt.

"Look, we got a problem," said Todd. "Johnson here managed to get the book confiscated by Jevicky."

Even at a distance through the trees, Lauren could see Gary's eyes widen in horror. "Jevicky has the book?"

"Yeah, but we're gonna get it back," Todd reassured him. "Tonight. You still got the key to the gym hall's side entrance?"

"You wanna break in and get it back?"

"You got a better idea?"

"Jevicky can't keep that book," said Brooke. "We have to get it back."

"Do you still have the key?" Todd pressed.

"Yeah, yeah, I still have it."

"Good. Then I'll come pick you up tonight at nine. Your old man give a shit about the curfew?"

"No, he's heading down to Sacramento to spend the weekend with Suzanne. He's on his way now."

"Good. Nine then."

"Hey, you guys, I really think we should destroy that book once we get it back," Gary said.

"Are you kidding?" Todd said. "That thing gives us the power of life and death! We could run this town if we wanted to!"

"That's insane, Todd," said Toby. "People are gonna get wise to us eventually."

"Yeah, I really think we should just get rid of it," Brooke agreed.

"You pussies!" Todd said. "We finally get our chance to get our own back on the losers in this town and you want to throw it all away."

"It's too dangerous!" said Gary. "And it's not just getting our own back! It's murder!"

"We can't keep using it, babe," said Brooke. "We'll get caught. And besides, the whole thing just creeps me out."

"Fine," Todd said reluctantly. "We get the book back and we burn it. But we'd just better make sure that there is nobody else we want out of the way first. Last call at the bar and all that."

It chilled Lauren to hear Todd talk so casually about murdering people and she realized that she believed them now, or at least believed that *they* believed they could kill people with a book of spells. She also realized that the conversation was over and, with alarm, saw that the four of them were heading back up the slope towards school. They would see her! She turned and moved as quickly and as silently back up the wooded slope as she could.

It was no good. She was too close and too visible in her pink sweater, and she heard the angry shouts behind her as they spotted her fleeing.

"It's that freak's daughter!" Brooke yelled. "Have you been spying on us, freak?"

"She is so fucking dead!" Todd bellowed.

Lauren believed he meant every word of that sentence and doubled her efforts to get back to the relative safety of school grounds. She panted as she scrambled up the slope, the books in her backpack banging against her spine, the strap slipping off her shoulder, hindering her.

She reached the school grounds, but most people had gone home, and she knew there would be nobody to protect her. She glanced behind her. Todd was way behind, puffing and panting, but Brooke and the other two boys were gaining on her fast. They wouldn't actually kill her on school grounds, would they? That she didn't know the answer to that question terrified her.

"Get her!" Brooke screamed and the two boys seemed to sprint ahead, spurred on by her words.

Lauren's only thought was to get inside the school and hope some teachers were still lurking about. As she approached the side entrance to the main building, she saw the door miraculously open and the figure of Mr. Hinzman appeared, a box of drama supplies in his hands. Lauren could have wept with relief.

"Hey, what's going on here?" Mr. Hinzman demanded as the two boys slid to a halt at a safe distance from Lauren with Brooke and Todd bringing up the rear. Mr. Hinzman looked from the four of them to Lauren, concern in his eyes. "Are these guys giving you a hard time?" he asked.

"Oh, it's nothing," Lauren said. She was thankful for his sudden appearance but wasn't about to rat on Brooke and her friends. Her life wouldn't be worth spit if she did that, not that it was worth much more than that anyway.

Mr. Hinzman wasn't convinced, and he glared at her four pursuers. "You kids shouldn't be on school property after the bell. Now, get off home right now."

Eyes shooting daggers at Lauren, Brooke and her friends slunk off without a word. Mr. Hinzman watched them leave and then turned to Lauren. "If those kids are bullying you, Lauren ..." he began.

"It's really nothing, Mr. Hinzman," she protested. "We were just playing around. Look, I should really get home."

"Yes, you should, Lauren. And remember the curfew."

"Yes, Mr. Hinzman."

"And promise me you'll tell me or one of the other teachers if those guys are taking things too far?"

"Yes, Mr. Hinzman."

He nodded and headed off to his car while Lauren reached into her pocket for her own keys. As she approached the Lipstads' old station wagon, she saw Todd's van roll out of the parking lot. Brooke was sitting in the passenger's seat, and she rolled the window down as they passed, glaring at Lauren and running her finger along her neck as if to say; 'you're dead!'

Lauren thanked her stars that it was her turn to have the car this week. She had no desire to walk home with Todd and Brooke cruising the streets looking for her.

CHAPTER 11

"I'm telling you, Lauren, that book of spells is what they're using to kill people!" Corey exclaimed. "And now they're gonna break into the school to get it back!"

Lauren instantly regretted telling Corey about what she had found out earlier that day. It was Friday night, and she was babysitting him, but they weren't doing any of the usual things they did like hide around the house with walkie talkies or watch old movies. Lauren had desperately wanted to tell somebody about what she had overheard and knew Mr. and Mrs. Lipstadt wouldn't believe her, and Harriet wouldn't be interested. She had no friends to talk to and so, perhaps selfishly, she had told Corey, a ten-year-old kid.

"I just can't believe it, though," Lauren said. "Books can't kill people."

"Well, *something* killed those people. And these friends of yours seem to think they're responsible."

"They're *not* my friends," Lauren protested. "And Mrs. Ross and all the others were killed by stabbing and strangulation. I don't see how a book of spells can do that to somebody. It could be that Brooke and Todd and the others are actually murdering these people and using this book as some kind of excuse. Jesus, I can't believe I'm talking about this with you!"

"Hey, I'm old enough to handle it. I know about way more creepy stuff than you, I bet. What time did they say they were going to break into the school?"

"Nine."

"That gives us half an hour."

She blinked at him. "Half an hour to do what?"

"Get down there and see for sure what they're up to!"

"You must be kidding! They nearly got their hands on me this afternoon in broad daylight. Who knows what they would do to me in an empty school after dark?"

"But you said yourself that Brooke threatened to kill you. What if they decide to unleash whatever cosmic forces they've harnessed on you?"

Lauren said nothing, a chill of fear settling in the pit of her stomach.

"You have one chance to stop them. If you could get your hands on that book, then who knows how many lives you could save?"

"I really should just call the police. I know that they're going to break into the school. That should be enough ..."

"The cops won't do anything! They might arrest them for breaking in but then they'll know it was you who ratted on them and they'll still have the book! You'll definitely be their next target if you don't get that book away from them!"

"And destroy it."

"Well, after we've looked through it of course."

She frowned at him. "You want to get your hands on it, don't you?"

"Only in the name of paranormal research," he shrugged.

"Well, forget it. Even if it's all phony, those guys are serious about it and something like that is too dangerous to keep around. It needs to be destroyed."

"You're thinking of going up to the school, aren't you?" He grinned at her, barely able to contain his excitement.

Lauren chewed on a hangnail. She couldn't believe she was considering this. She should call the cops, but Corey was right. That wouldn't work. Nothing would work, especially not sitting here and hoping it would all go away. If Brooke and the others truly had the power to kill people, then she *had* to do something to stop them.

Brooke's hate-filled face from the passenger seat of Todd's van that afternoon flashed into her mind, the finger slicing across her throat, razor-like. Brooke had wanted Lauren dead for years now. She blamed her for the murder of her sister and had made her life a living hell just to show it. Now, she might have the power to kill her from a distance with no repercussions. Lauren knew Brooke would have no qualms about putting her in the ground if she could.

An anger swelled in her chest when she thought of how Brooke had tried to blame the most recent murders on her dad when it had been her and her friends who were responsible all along. Brooke had *known* that it hadn't been Anthony Stevens who had murdered those people and yet she had still been happy to victimize her and treat her like she was somehow complicit because her dead father had murdered a bunch of people five years ago. Now Brooke was the murderer and Lauren found that she was determined to stop her from getting away with it.

"You're right," she said at last. "I'm going to have to go up there to the school."

"All right!" Corey yelled. "Let's get going! We don't have much time."

"Wait a minute. 'We'? You're staying right here, mister!"

Corey's face fell. "No way, Lauren! You have to let me come!"

"This isn't a game, Corey! These people are dangerous. Killers, even."

"You can't leave me here on my own!" Corey said, stamping his foot angrily. "You're my babysitter! What if I electrocute myself with the toaster? What if there's a fire? You'd never forgive yourself and that's before we get to all the legal stuff about negligence ..."

"OK, OK!" Lauren snapped, knowing she was beaten. "You can come. But you stick with me and do exactly what I tell you!"

Corey beamed at her and they went to get their jackets.

The school gymnasium echoed as the key rattled in the lock, its cavernous and dim interior an open mouth, gaping and vacant. The door swung open, and the four intruders entered, gazing at a place at once so familiar to them but given an otherworldly sheen by the lateness of the hour. Ordinarily filled with the sound of sneakers squeaking on polished wood and the slam of basketballs, this somber chamber was as silent as a tomb, small particles of undisturbed dust drifting in the moonlight shining through the high windows.

"All right!" said Todd in a whisper. "I knew that key of yours would come in handy, Gary."

"You don't have to whisper, Todd," said Toby. "We've got the whole school to ourselves."

Todd held his hands up, the fingers made into devil horns, and whooped with exhilaration. "Fuck, yeah!", his voice resounding around the gymnasium and bouncing off the walls.

"We should totally party while we're here," said Brooke. "None of our parents know we're out so we have all night to go wild!"

"Yeah, we could totally trash this place, and nobody would even know it was us!" said Todd.

"Let's just get that book and get out of here," said Gary.

"What's the matter with you, man?" Todd said, punching his friend on the shoulder. "You've turned into a real wuss lately. We'll get the book, so just relax huh? But we are definitely gonna party while we're here! I'll get some beers from the van."

He headed back out while the other three stood around looking at the gloomy gymnasium. Brooke rubbed her arms. "School sure is creepy after dark," she said.

"Hey, don't worry," said Toby with a small grin. "We're the scariest things here!"

Todd returned with a six pack and slammed the gymnasium door behind him with a deafening clang. He broke off cans for each of them and they popped the tops and guzzled beer as they headed through the echoing gymnasium towards the double doors that led to the rest of the school.

"Jevicky will have that book somewhere in his office," said Gary. "I hope we don't need a key to get in there. I only have my mom's old one for the side entrance."

"If it's locked, we'll just bust in there," said Todd, taking another gulp from his beer can. "It's not like anybody will know we were here."

They wandered down the deserted hallways, past the olive-green lockers and twinkling trophy cabinet, to the teachers' corridor where Principal Jevicky's office door stood at the end with its frosted glass panel. Todd tried the door handle and grinned as it swung open.

Giddy at the prospect of being in the principal's office when nobody else was around and no promise of reprisal, they sauntered in and began investigating the room thoroughly. Drawers were flung open, trophies and family photographs examined and tossed carelessly aside.

"Ugly kids," Todd remarked at a framed photograph of Principal Jevicky with his wife and two kids on a beach somewhere. He hurled the frame with disgust at a bookshelf and the glass shattered.

This spontaneous act of destruction spurred the others on, and they began ransacking the office with more reckless abandon, pulling drawers completely out of the desk and riffling through the papers within, swiping books off the shelves and rummaging through the filing cabinet.

"Hey, check out that old booze hound," said Toby as he discovered a half-empty bottle of scotch in a bottom drawer."

"Score!" said Todd. "Gimmie!"

Toby handed the bottle over and, screwing off the cap, Todd took a swig and then passed it to Gary, grimacing at the fiery liquor.

"Where the fuck is the book?" Brooke demanded, searching through the student records and other paperwork of the filing cabinet. "It has to be in here somewhere."

"Whatever, this place is boring," said Todd. "Anybody hungry? I bet we could swipe some of those chocolate puddings from the cafeteria."

"What if the book isn't here?" Gary asked, a hint of panic entering his voice. "What if Jevicky took it home with him or gave it to somebody else?"

"Then we're fucked," said Todd. "But I'm hungry. Brooke, you coming with?"

Brooke shrugged. "Sure. But you guys keep looking."

"Shit!" said Gary as Todd and Brooke headed off towards the cafeteria. He looked around at the mess they had made of the office. "It's gotta be here somewhere!"

"It must be," said Toby, "But I gotta take a leak."

"You're all just leaving me here to find the damn thing on my own?" Gary exploded. "Am I the only one who wants to get that thing back so we don't all end up in deep shit?"

"Relax, Gary," said Toby. "We have all night to find it. It'll be here somewhere. I'll be right back."

Still not quite able to believe what she was doing, Lauren pulled up in the school parking lot and switched off the engine. They had taken the Lipstadt's station wagon from the driveway, silently sneaking off with it while Mr. and Mrs. Lipstadt watched TV, the flickering set casting dancing shadows against the window.

Lauren glanced at Corey in the passenger seat. The damn kid was having the time of his life. Sneaking out at night to break into the high school while there was some occult spell book on the loose? She must be crazy to bring him, but she knew she couldn't have left him alone.

"All right," she said. "Gary said he had a key to the gymnasium's side door. That's just around that corner. I don't suppose I can convince you to stay in the car?"

"Not a chance!" Corey said, his eyes alight with mischief. "I'm with you every step of the way."

"Just make sure that you are. No wandering off and no doing anything unless I tell you first, OK?"

He saluted her. "Affirmative!"

They got out of the car and wandered around the side of the school to where the gymnasium jutted out behind the main building. As they approached the side door, Lauren could see that it was open. Those jerks hadn't even closed it behind them.

Being in the school after dark was always a weird feeling. Lauren had done it enough times as a member of the drama club, but she never lost the strange sense of an empty building haunted by the laughter and voices of generations of students. These walls had witnessed countless happy celebrations, teenage romances, bullied kids, broken hearts and shattered dreams. Her parents had known these walls as their own and had walked down those same hallways as she had done, times beyond number.

And so had Anthony Stevens.

She hated this school and the stranglehold it seemed to have over her life. The misery of her own existence had been born in these hallways long before she had even been conceived.

"Where are we going?" Corey whispered as he padded alongside her.

"The principal's office," she whispered back. "That's where they would look for the book."

As they rounded the hallway, the gloom seemed to stretch ahead of them, the regular rows of lockers making the corridor seem longer than it actually was. Way down at the far end, silhouetted against the moonlight streaming in from the window behind it, something moved. Lauren's heart skipped a beat as she realized that somebody was at the far end of the hallway and that they had seen them.

CHAPTER 12

The cafeteria was even more eerie than the gymnasium after dark. The shadows were deep beneath the rows of tables, the moonlight reflecting off their flat surfaces. The vending machines with their bright, fluorescent logos hummed away in the corner, the only noise that cut through the utter stillness.

"Come on," Todd said, heading over to the empty glass counters. "This way."

He and Brooke clambered over the counter and pushed open the swing door to the kitchens. A pitch-black void opened before them. Todd reached his arm around the doorway and ran his fingers along the tiles looking for a light switch. He couldn't find one.

"Guess we'll just have to feel our way about," he said.

"Screw that, I'm not going in there!" said Brooke.

"Come on, babe, I'm here to protect you!" Todd said, giving her a wink.

"I'm serous, Todd, I'm not going into that pitch black kitchen!"

"Fine, wait here then. I'll find the puddings."

Brooke sighed. If Todd wasn't thinking about beer or sex then he was thinking about food. Why did his tubby ass need to eat chocolate pudding in the middle of the night anyway? She was fine with trashing Jevicky's office and having a party but she'd feel a lot better about it if they stuck together and found that book first.

Todd vanished into the gloom making goofy 'weee-oooo' noises.

"Quit it, Todd!" Brooke snapped.

"Chill, babe. I found the refrigerator."

The door to the gargantuan refrigerator squeaked open and a yellowish light spilled out, illuminating Todd as he stood before his bounty. "Oh, man!" he said and started helping himself to chocolate pudding tubs, pilling them up in his arms.

Brooke jumped as she heard a noise in the darkness of the cafeteria at her back. She spun around and scanned the gloom. Over by the entrance, she could see a figure standing there. "Gary?" She called. There came no reply. "Toby?"

"Those guys out there?" Todd yelled from the kitchen. "Tell them to get their asses in here and help me carry this shit. We are gonna have a feast!"

But Brooke had the sickening feeling that the figure who had entered the cafeteria was neither Gary nor Toby. It stared at her for a moment and then, with a sudden lurch, it shambled forward in a gait she instantly recognized. There was a clatter as it bumped into a chair, sending it tumbling to one side and, as it passed into the light from the windows, Brooke saw its face.

She screamed. Anthony Stevens, the zombified, mind-controlled corpse of Anthony Stevens, was here in the school with them and it was coming towards her, single eye livid and jelly-like, shriveled gums and withered tongue slavering idiotically.

Brooke backed into the kitchen, hands over her mouth, circling the large island of hotplates and worksurfaces to reach Todd. She slammed the refrigerator door shut, knocking several tubs of chocolate pudding from Todd's arms.

"Hey, what did you do that for?" he demanded.

They had been plunged into darkness by the closing of the door and Brooke clung to him, hissing into his ear; "Shhh! He's here!"

"Who?" Todd dumbly exclaimed.

"That that ... *thing*! Anthony Stevens!"

"What!" Todd suddenly hissed, understanding her sudden need for silence at last. He let the pudding tubs tumble from his arms and grabbed Brooke, holding her in front of him like a human shield.

"What are you doing!" Brooke gasped.

"He won't hurt you, you're one of the ... the ... ones who made the sacrifice! But he'll kill me, babe! You remember how he went for me at the park? You gotta keep him away from me!"

"Be quiet!" Brooke urged him. "He might not find us!"

There was a clatter in the serving area as the undead mass-murderer hauled himself over the counter. Brooke and Todd held their breaths as his figure appeared in the doorway to the kitchen, limned in the moonlight from behind. He halted and seemed to be scanning the gloom for them. Could he see in the dark? Could he sense them hiding in the shadows?

Please go away, please go away! Brooke prayed.

But the killer moved into the kitchen and was swallowed by the darkness. They could no longer see him and a cold terror gripped Brooke's heart with the knowledge that *he* was in there with them, and they had no idea if he was close to them or not.

She tugged on Todd's arm and felt that he was stiff with terror. If they couldn't see Anthony Stevens, then he probably couldn't see them, and that meant that they could reach the doorway undetected. Slowly, *painfully* slowly, they edged around the island, following the wall towards that bright rectangle of salvation.

They both froze as the door to the refrigerator slowly creaked open.

Yellow light flooded the room. Brooke and Todd were like deer caught in the headlights, pressed up against the tiles, their shadows plastered behind them. Anthony Stevens stood by the refrigerator, looking at them, half in shadow, half in light, his black eyes like a death's head focused on them.

"Run!" Brooke cried and they bolted towards the doorway.

Anthony Stevens, with a speed that defied his rotten and dead form, rushed around the island and put himself between them and their escape. They cowered from him, looking around desperately for another way out. The door at their back led to the walk-in freezer and the rear entrance which would be locked. There was no way out but past the killer who stood in front of them.

Anthony Stevens pulled a large meat cleaver from the knife block on the island and moved towards them. The light from the refrigerator glinted along its razor-sharp stainless-steel edge. Brooke screamed. Todd gibbered with terror. Anthony lunged.

Brooke raised her arm to shield herself, resigned to her grisly fate while Todd cowered behind her. But instead of striking, the killer grabbed Brooke roughly by the arm and hauled her out of the way before swinging the meat cleaver at Todd.

It was Todd he wanted.

Barely able to believe that she was still alive, Brooke scuttled past the killer's legs and hovered by the doorway. She could run. She *should* run, but what about Todd?

The killer had missed with his first swipe and Todd was backing away from him as he advanced for a second try. Brooke screamed as the meat cleaver whistled through the air, nearly scalping Todd and clicking off the tiles, sending a chip flying.

In desperation, Brooke seized a knife from the same chopping block Anthony Stevens had taken the meat cleaver and ran at the killer, screaming all the while. She slammed the knife's point into his back. The blade sank in easily and noiselessly through the rotten flesh. The killer straightened but uttered no sound or any other sign of discomfort. He registered that he had been stabbed but seemed to see this as a mild annoyance. He turned and shoved Brooke roughly away from him. She fell, striking her head against the tiled floor.

Looking up, dizzily, she saw the killer pull the knife from his abdomen and let it fall to the floor with a clatter. There was no gush of blood, but Brooke could see that the knife blade was coated in a thick, syrupy substance, dark like blood, but congealed and sticky.

Then, Anthony returned his focus on Todd, swinging the meat cleaver again, this time making contact with Todd's upraised arm. Todd screamed as the blade bit through flesh and crunched into bone. The killer jerked the cleaver free, yanking Todd's partially severed arm to one side, leaving him open for the next attack.

Brooke screamed again as the meat cleaver swung down, embedding itself in Todd's face. The force of the blow sank him to his knees, and he looked up at his killer dumbly, almost cross-eyed with the cleaver wedged into the bridge of his nose. A thin trickle of blood ran down the edge of the blade.

With a savage wrench, the killer worked the cleaver free and then brought it down again on the top of Todd's head, and again, and again, each time working deeper into the skull to get at the brain within.

Brooke watched in appalled horror as her boyfriend's blood sprayed up in wheeling jets every time the killer whipped the cleaver up for another blow, its blade coated in gore and fragments of skull. Todd's face was a bloody ruin and, as he sank mercifully out of sight behind the island, Brooke knew that he was dead and there was nothing more she could do.

Getting to her feet, the wet squelch of cleaver striking flesh echoing in her ears, she ran out of the kitchen, slid over the counter, and made for the doors, her body wracked with sobs.

"What the hell are you doing here?" the figure at the end of the hallway cried.

Lauren recognized Toby's voice. She hadn't had much of a plan, but she had hoped their presence wouldn't be discovered so soon. Now what?

"We've come to stop you and your little cult, freak-o!" Corey piped up by her side.

Toby approached them, his eyes wide in the light, matched by his teeth. He was grinning. "Oh?" he said. "And just what exactly do you know about me and my little cult?"

"We know you've been killing people," said Lauren. "And something about a book of spells."

The grin remained on Toby's face, rictus like. "You do, do you? And where did you get a crazy notion like that ... oh, wait! Now I know! I remember this little squirt hanging around the pizza parlor the other week. He's your little snoop, huh?"

Lauren reached her arm around and moved Corey behind her, as if to shield him from the crazed satanist.

"Hey, who are you talking to, Johnson?" came Gary's voice as he appeared at the door to Principal Jevicky's office. "Oh, shit!" he said as he saw Lauren and Corey.

"The Scooby gang here decided to interfere," said Toby.

"Hey, you guys can't tell anybody we were here tonight," said Gary.

"No shit," said Toby,

118

"You're breaking in too," Gary added. "You'll be in just as much trouble as us."

"But we're not breaking in to murder people," said Lauren.

"What?" said Gary, affecting outrage. "Who's murdering anybody? There's nobody here but us!"

"They know about the book," said Toby.

Gary's face fell. "Shit! Oh, shit!"

"Yeah," Toby agreed. "Which is bad news for them if they don't keep their mouths shut. It'll happen when you least expect it. When you're walking home from school or relaxing in front of the TV. Or even when you're asleep in your bed. You think anyone will believe it was us who killed you? We won't even be at the scene. It's like pushing a button on a remote control!"

"So you're just admitting it?" Lauren asked, genuinely surprised to find that it was all true and not just a misunderstanding. These maniacs were actually using black magic to kill people. How it all worked was something she didn't understand. She didn't see how reading magic spells could cause people to get strangled and stabbed without some third party playing a part ...

"He's here!" came a scream from further down the hallway in the direction of the cafeteria. The four of them jumped and turned to see a hysterical Brooke running towards them, her face sheeted in tears. "He's here!" she wailed.

CHAPTER 13

"*Who's* here?" Gary demanded.

"He's here in the school and he killed Todd!"

"Who?"

"That *thing*! Anthony Stevens!"

Lauren felt her guts twist into a knot. The final piece of the puzzle revealed itself, but she wasn't sure how it fitted. It couldn't be true, could it? Could her father, whom she had tried so hard to believe was dead, be up and about and murdering people again? Could her worst nightmare be a reality? And how was he connected to Brooke and Todd and the others?

"Todd's dead?" Gary said, his face pasty in the moonlight.

"He butchered him! He hacked him to pieces in the kitchen!"

"Why the hell is *he* here?" Gary asked. "He's supposed to go after the people we tell him to, not follow us about! What's going on, Toby? Why the fuck is he here?"

"Relax," said Toby. "Todd never made the sacrifice, remember? He wasn't one of the circle. He was never protected like we are."

"But why kill Todd?" Brooke whimpered.

"I don't know. Maybe he just kills anything in his path. Like those campers. We never sent him after those two. Maybe he just came upon them the night we resurrected him. Maybe we're the only three people in the whole world who are safe from him."

"Wait a minute," said Lauren, her heart pounding at the implications of all that she was hearing. "Are you saying that you guys have resurrected Anthony Stevens and have been using him to kill people?"

"I guess it doesn't matter much if you know the truth now," said Toby. "Yeah, we control your pop like a puppet on strings. He's been very useful to us."

"Why the fuck are *you* here?" Brooke said, forgetting her panic for as long as it took to spit her usual venom at Lauren.

"Snooping on us," said Toby. "We'll deal with them, don't sweat it."

"We have to find that book," said Brooke, palming away the last of her tears. "It's the only way we can destroy him."

"Fuck that, I'm getting out of here!" Gary whimpered. "I'm not sticking around to find out if I'm safe from that thing! I've let you drag me into this too deep already."

"It's your fucking book, man," said Toby.

"Nobody knows that! It's not like my name is on the fucking thing! I'm splitting!"

They watched as he turned from them and ran off down the corridor, back towards the gymnasium.

"Let him go," said Toby. "We don't need him. Let's just keep looking for the book."

"Promise me, Toby," Brooke pleaded. "Promise me that when we find it, we'll use it to put Anthony Stevens back in the ground and then destroy it for good?"

"Sure," said Toby. He put his arm around Brooke and Lauren could see that she shrank even from that small comfort. She could tell that Toby freaked her out, just like he freaked everybody out.

He looked briefly hurt but recovered himself quickly and glared at Lauren and Corey. "You guys better stick close too, with Anthony Stevens roaming the school. Brooke and I are protected but you two aren't."

"What do you mean you and Brooke are protected?" Corey asked,

"It was us and Gary who summoned Anthony Stevens from beyond the grave, squirt," said Toby. "We control him. We all lost somebody at his hands five years ago. Todd didn't. He never made the sacrifice to bring him back."

"Sacrifice?" Lauren asked, unnerved even further by the implications of the word.

"Little trinkets belonging to the victims," Toby explained. "There is always a sacrifice to be made."

"That's why we need to find it," said Brooke. "It's the only thing that connects us to the murders. And it's the only way we can undo what we've done."

"You can't undo what you've done!" Lauren exploded at her. "People are dead because of you guys! There's no taking that back! And you let everybody believed that my father was back, killing people!"

"No word a lie," said Toby.

"You ruined my life!" Lauren screamed. She felt ready to hit Brooke, to pummel her with her fists for everything she had done to her over the past five years. "You blamed me for it all. You all blamed me!"

"Yeah?" said Brooke, her misery snapping suddenly into a vicious rage. "So what? It *was* your father who killed all those people. He murdered my sister. I ruined *your* life? Your dad ruined mine before I was out of eighth grade! So, yeah, we used your dad's moldy old corpse to even the score a little. So fucking what?"

"Ladies, ladies," said Toby, holding his hands up. "Let's not tear each other's throats out. Now, I suggest we go back into Jevicky's office and carry on the search. The book must be in there somewhere."

Lauren and Brooke continued to stare daggers at each other, tears in their eyes. Lauren was the first to look away, not because she was unable to face her bully after all these years, but she knew she had to focus on the present for her own sake and for Corey's sake. She was responsible for his safety. Her father was somewhere in this building, or what was left of him, and she had to do what she could to stop him.

Gary knew he was being a coward, but he no longer cared. He hadn't wanted any of this. All he had done was steal a weird notebook he thought the others might find interesting. He hadn't wanted to raise the dead and he certainly hadn't wanted to kill anybody. That was all Todd and Toby. They had caused all of this and now Todd was dead.

He was bailing. He didn't care about finding the book. Let Toby look for it if he wanted. He'd wished he'd never seen the damn thing. Who had he wanted to kill? What had all this black magic bullshit done for him except drag him into something so nightmarish he didn't know how to get out of it? The cops would be asking a lot of questions about the break in and about Todd's murder, but nothing could come back on him. He hadn't done any of this and if they asked, he would just say that he was only a bystander. Let Toby take the fall, it was all his stupid idea anyway.

He made his way across the empty gymnasium to the door. Grabbing the handle, he gave it a wrench. It was locked! Who the hell had locked the door? He fumbled in his pocket for the key and realized that he didn't have it. Fresh panic gripped him with the knowledge that he was locked inside the building with that monster. Where the hell was the key?

He frantically worked the door handle, hoping to force it open and the rattling that echoed around the gymnasium made him oblivious to the footsteps approaching him from behind. A heavy hand landed on his shoulder, spinning him around to face the rotten, maggot-ravaged visage of Anthony Stevens.

A cry of terror choked Gary. The sudden burst of adrenaline coursing through his veins broke through the paralyzing fear quick enough for him to duck the savage swing of the meat cleaver which embedded itself in the door behind where his head had been a split second before. While the killer tried to work it free, Gary bolted towards the supply room where the school's athletic equipment was kept.

There was a door at the back of the supply room which led to the sports field and Gary knew it would be locked. He tried it anyway, slamming his full weight against it and jerking the handle up and down. With a sob he knew that he was trapped and looked around for something with which to defend himself.

The killer was moving towards the supply room, and, in the gloom, Gary spotted the rack of javelins. Seizing one, he held it out, ready to jab his pursuer in the guts. Anthony Stevens did not slacken his pace as he entered the room, the meat cleaver held above his head, still red and sticky with Todd's blood.

Gary screamed and thrust with his javelin as the killer approached. The tip pricked Anthony's chest and he did not even register the wound, instead pushing himself forward, impaling himself on the javelin to get closer to Gary.

The meat cleaver swished through the air and Gary was forced to let go of his weapon and back up, mere inches of empty space between his throat and the glistening steel. Why was this happening to him? Wasn't he supposed to be safe from Anthony Stevens? Why was this undead maniac so fixated on killing him? It didn't make any sense.

He had little time to ponder the questions racing through his head as Anthony was pulling the javelin back through his body. The bloodied meat cleaver dropped from his hand as he turned the spear around, half of it sticky with whatever passed for his own blood, and gripped it with both hands, ready to thrust at his prey.

Gary desperately tried to move out of the way of the jabbing spear, pulling down whatever he could lay his hands on to hinder the killer. A net of basketballs opened and spilled across the room. A rack of bows and quivers tumbled down on top of Anthony, tangling up his javelin arm. As he thrashed and flailed about, he stepped on a basketball and his legs shot out from under him and he landed heavily amid the detritus.

Seizing his chance to escape, Gary hopped over the wreckage of sports gear and bolted from the room. He pelted across the gymnasium towards the double doors and almost made it before the bloodied javelin thudded into the wood of the door. He slid to a halt and looked behind him. Anthony had emerged from the storage room and had a bunch of javelins in his left fist. Plucking another one, he drew his arm back and took aim at Gary.

Knowing he wouldn't make it through the doors without being impaled, Gary dove to one side as the javelin sailed through the air and clattered across the polished wood of the floor. He was a human target in the wide, open space and there was only one area of the gymnasium that offered any cover. He ran towards the bleachers, ducking as another javelin whistled overhead and struck the far wall.

He scrambled under the bleachers, peering through them at the killer who had only one javelin left. This was little comfort to Gary as he watched him approach, javelin held low for thrusting. He was stuck under the bleachers, and they offered little protection from the long reach of the javelin.

He rolled as it slid between the seats. He could see the killer's mud-encrusted boots on the bottom bench as he leaned forward to try and skewer him again and again. Crawling on his hands and knees, Gary made for the far end of the bleachers, near the doors. He cried out as the javelin slid across his back, cutting a long line through his shirt and skin.

Reaching the end of the bleachers, he was up and running for the door while the killer was still poking about at the darkness, trying to nail his target. He jerked upright and spun around as the sound of Gary hauling open the heavy doors reached his ears. Sobbing, Gary slipped through them and slammed the door closed behind him, wishing there was some way to bolt it.

He turned and had a split second to consider his next move. A long hallway stretched ahead of him. He wouldn't reach the end by the time Anthony Stevens came through the doors and hurled his javelin the length of the hallway. Having no desire to be struck in the back, Gary lurched into the boys' locker room on his left. He would hide in there and hope the killer would pass by.

He wove his way between the aisles of lockers and benches and slumped down onto his haunches behind the end of one of them. His heart was beating at a frantic pace. Cold sweat prickled his face and his fear barely let him feel the hot line of pain where the javelin had grazed his back.

He heard the doors to the gymnasium clang open and closed his eyes, praying to whoever might be listening that the killer would walk on by.

A long time seemed to pass during which Gary began to think that his prayers had been answered and he had given his pursuer the slip. But then a footfall echoed around the locker room and his heart sank. The killer was in there with him.

He could hear his footsteps as he moved past the rows of lockers at the other end of the room. No doubt Anthony was checking each aisle. When he was done, he would come around and check the aisles from the other end. He had to get out of there, but it was best to do so quietly.

Too scared to even breathe, Toby waited until the footsteps had nearly reached the far corner of the room. Judging that the killer had passed his position, he crept across to the next row of lockers, glancing down the aisle as he did so. There was no sign of the killer. He also could no longer hear him. The footsteps had stopped.

Was he waiting? If Gary made a break for it, he was confident that he'd be able to get out of the locker room alive but that would mean blowing his cover and having the killer on his heels once more. But he couldn't wait around forever. The killer would check every corner of the room, behind every locker, until he found him.

Keeping low, he moved to the next row of lockers, and then the next. His confidence building, he increased his speed, although still trying to make as little noise as possible. He waited at the last row of lockers. The door was just on the other side. He was almost there! He licked his dry lips and tensed himself to make his break for freedom. With any luck, he could get out of there without the killer noticing. Stevens might spend another few minutes searching the locker room, by which time Gary could find a much better hiding spot somewhere in the school.

He rose to his feet and rounded the corner, a burst of speed powering him on ... right onto the end of the killer's javelin as Anthony Stevens rounded the corner to meet him.

He gasped as he felt his breath stolen from his lungs and a sharp, ugly pain deep in his belly. He looked down at the javelin which had skewered him and then up at the face of his murderer. Anthony Stevens was no pretty picture at any distance, but close up, Gary could see the holes in his flesh the worms had left, the jellified eyes through which he could somehow still see. The stink of rot and decay filled his nostrils and he felt himself gagging, though that could have been the blood pooling in his stomach from the internal bleeding caused by the javelin piercing his innards.

His whole body convulsed, and blood rose up his throat and erupted from his lips. It was over. He was dying and there was nothing he could do about it. No more running. No more hiding. In a way, it was almost a relief.

And with the peaceful acceptance of death, one question which had been niggling the back of his consciousness through his frantic last moments rose to the forefront of his mind. What had happened to the key and who had locked the door?

Then he remembered. He had placed the key on the edge of Jevicky's desk when they had started trashing his office. He didn't remember seeing it after that. Surely, he would have noticed it when he left? Unless somebody else had taken it ...?

Then it hit him.

Toby.

Anthony wrenched the javelin out of his gut with a horrible sucking feeling and then, as Gary was in the process of toppling forward, he jammed it up under his chin, lifting him off his feet, the sharp point erupting from the top of his skull before embedding itself in the ceiling.

The killer let go and stood back to admire his handiwork. Gary dangled from the ceiling, like a limp fish from a hook, blood running from the holes on the top of his head and below his chin, down the length of the javelin to drip onto the tiled floor.

CHAPTER 14

They had ransacked Principal Jevicky's office from top to bottom and still hadn't found the book. It seemed hopeless. Brooke and Lauren said nothing to each other as they searched, the two mortal enemies curiously bonded as they worked towards a mutual goal. Corey had taken it upon himself to stand guard at the doorway and let them know if there was any sign of Anthony Stevens.

Lauren was still struggling to believe it all. It seemed too much like an elaborate prank at her expense. Was her father really stalking the hallways of the school? Had he really returned, called back from beyond the grave by these four maniacs?

Make that three, she thought when she remembered that Todd was dead.

There was no way that Brooke was that good an actress. She had been positively hysterical over her boyfriend's death. But had it really been Anthnoy Stevens, the bogeyman of Crimson Bay, who had killed him? There was still so much about all this that she had trouble accepting.

"Man, the book isn't here!" said Toby as he hurled a bundle of papers across the room in frustration. "I say we cut out of here and head home."

"What about Todd?" Brooke said, looking like she was about to cry again.

"We let him take the blame for breaking in here," Toby said. "There's no way we can cover up his death. He broke in, trashed Jevicky's office and then got killed by Anthony Stevens. Let the cops puzzle that one out. There's nothing that puts us here tonight."

"Jesus, how can you be so callous about Todd's death?" said Brooke.

"I'll be honest, Brooke, I never liked the guy," Toby replied. "And you were way too good for him."

"Look, I thought you desperately wanted that book back," said Lauren. "I thought it was evidence that tied you guys to the murders."

"Why do you care?" asked Brooke. "What are you even doing here anyway? Why do you want to find the book?"

"I just want all this killing to stop," said Lauren. "And if it is my father ... well, I just want *him* stopped."

"Well, if we can't find the book, we can't find it," Toby snapped. "You wanna stay here and look all night with your dad wandering around?"

"I don't want to stay here another second," said Brooke.

"Then let's split. Say, you don't suppose that dope Gary locked us in, do you?"

Fresh concern enveloped Lauren and Brooke. "He wouldn't," said Brooke.

"The state he was in, I don't know what he might have done," said Toby. "Let's go check."

They slipped out of the study and made their way back towards the gymnasium. They walked single file, with Toby in the lead and Lauren at the back, each of them glancing at the shadows, nervously.

As they reached the end of the hallway that led down to the gymnasium, Toby halted dead in his tracks. "Oh, fuck!" he said.

The others bumped into him from behind. Peering down the dim corridor, they could see what had made him come to such an abrupt halt. A figure was coming towards them, tall and ragged. The moonlight shining in through the side windows revealed his face in patches of light and dark. Pale and wrinkled skin surrounded dark, skull-like eyes and a rictus grin of broken and yellowed teeth flashed a deathly smile.

And all at once, Lauren knew the nightmare was real. Despite the ravages of the grave, she recognized the man approaching them. She remembered how he had dragged her to his house in the woods, how he had made her sit at the dining table with the corpse of her mother like some sick parody of a happy family. Most of all, she remembered how he had pursued her as she had tried to flee, the hard grip of his hands on her legs as she had squirmed through the window ...

Toby suddenly grabbed Brooke around the middle and pulled her to one side. He flung out a finger at Lauren and Corey. "They're the ones who must die next!" he yelled. "Kill them! I command you to kill them both!"

"What are you doing?" Brooke demanded as he manhandled her back the way they had come.

"Come on, Brooke, we don't need to see this!" he said.

Brooke tried to fight him but her fear of the figure that was striding down the hallway towards them weakened her resolve and she let herself be dragged away.

"Toby, you fucking bastard!" Lauren yelled, but they were gone, and she and Corey were alone as the killer bore down on them.

Lauren grabbed Corey's hand and they took off down the hallway which ran around the main building in a loop. If they could outrun her father, then they could find some place to hide.

As they rounded the corner, Lauren realized that she had made a terrible mistake. A set of fire doors sealed the east wing of the school from the west, and she knew from experience that the janitor locked them every night. *Oh, Lauren, you fool!* she thought as she and Corey slammed against the fire doors and tried to budge them. They were trapped.

Anthony Stevens rounded the corridor and Corey cowered behind Lauren, a small whimper escaping his lips. Lauren hated herself for bringing him with her. She should have left him at home. Now he was going to die because of her.

Her father lumbered towards them, and Lauren was hit by the wall of stench. His rotten flesh soured the air. His bony hands, stripped of skin and flesh in several areas, reached out, groping. Lauren braced herself, holding Corey behind her with both hands, determined to die first. Anthony lunged, intent on killing her with his bare hands.

And then, he halted.

Lauren, who had squeezed her eyes shut, opened them a sliver. The putrid, worm-eaten face of her father was inches from her own. No breath escaped his lips or the gaping hole where his nose had once been, but her own nostrils were filled with his stink. She gazed into those jellified eyes and wondered what the hell he was waiting for.

Something had definitely made him halt his murderous impulse and he gazed at Lauren with that expressionless face of death. Did he recognize her? Was there still a functioning brain in there with actual memories? The thought that this creature remembered her was almost even more horrific than being pursued by a mindless killing machine.

Anthony's shriveled lips moved, as if trying to form words. A harsh, papery whistle emitted from his throat, suggesting that there was little left of his vocal cords.

"St ... stay away!" Lauren commanded him, wondering if she was pushing her luck to give this thing that had been her father orders.

Anthony looked from her to Corey who was peeking out from behind her. She could see that he wanted to kill the young boy but, for reasons only he understood, he was unable to kill her to get at him.

Keeping herself between Corey and her father, Lauren edged around him, hoping that she could use his momentary stalling to escape. There was clearly some battle of wills going on inside that cracked and rotten skull and she didn't want to wait around to find out which side would win.

He watched her dumbly, reaching out with groping claws, as she circled him and began backing back down the hallway. He followed them and, once they had reached the corner, Lauren murmured some instructions to Corey.

"When I say so, I want you to run into the auditorium. It's the double doors in the middle of the hallway on your left."

"What about you?" Corey said.

"I'll hold his attention, now just do as I say. Go! Now!"

Corey took off like a rabbit and Lauren saw Anthony take his eye off her to glance at him and then turn his focus back on her, confirming that it was her he was most interested in.

She heard the clang of the auditorium doors as Corey did as she had told him. Those doors could be locked from the inside and there were several other exits leading to different parts of the school. She continued to back away and her father followed her step by step, looking all the while like he was about to lunge. She didn't know how fast this decrepit corpse could move, but she wasn't going to test it until she was close enough to the auditorium.

As she saw the doors in the tail of her eye, she pressed herself up against them and felt them give just a little. With a sudden movement, she pushed herself through and tried to slam them shut after her. Anthony lunged for her and hit the door as it closed, the force of the impact nearly knocking Lauren backwards.

She hurled herself against it, pushing Anthony back. A clawed hand swiped around the edge of the door and tried to reach for her arms. Corey, who had been hanging back, ran forward to join Lauren in trying to get the door closed. Between the two of them they were able to squash Anthony's arm until they heard the bone crack.

He gave no cry of pain and Lauren wondered if he felt any at all. But the arm was hastily withdrawn, its owner perhaps sensing that it was injured, and they were able to press the door closed at last. Lauren grabbed the cross bar and jerked it up, locking it.

In a hallway on the other side of the school, Brooke squirmed and hit at her captor.

"Stop!" she yelled as Toby continued to manhandle her. "Get your fucking hands off me!"

He eventually relented and she shook herself free of him. "Relax," he said. "It had to be done. I had to tie up those loose ends, they could have ratted us out. It's just us now."

"What do you mean, 'just us'? What about Gary?"

"Oh, I have a feeling he won't be saying anything to anybody."

"He ran out! He's probably calling the cops right now!"

"Not without the key to unlock the side door, he won't be," said Toby, pulling the key from his jeans pocket and dangling it in front of Brooke.

"You ... you have the key?" she asked. "But the door ...?"

"I locked it when I pretended to go take a leak. I couldn't have anybody running out on us. Not tonight when it all ends."

"Oh, my God!" said Brooke, covering her mouth with her hand. "You turned that monster on Todd and Gary! *You* killed them!"

Toby shrugged and gave her an apologetic grin. "Gary was a loose cannon. He was never gonna hold out and Todd? Jesus, Brooke, how could you be with that guy? He treated you like dirt. Every day I had to watch him paw you with his fat, grubby hands. And he was never going to give up, you know that right? He was a maniac who wanted to kill anybody who crossed him. He had to be taken out of the picture. *Permanently.*

"But ... the book ... How did you ...?"

"You mean this book?" He pulled the notebook from the inside pocket of his jacket. "I had it all along. Jevicky never took it. I lied about that, but I had to have some reason to lure Todd and Gary to the school after dark. I considered sending Anthony Stevens after them separately, like we did with my stepdad and Mrs. Ross, but I figured that it was best to get them both done on the same night. I couldn't have one of them getting wise to me."

"And ... me?"

He looked shocked at the suggestion. "I would never do anything to hurt you, Brooke. I *love* you. I did all this for us, so we could be together."

"Wh ... what?"

"You and me, Brooke! We're the only ones who know about the book, about Anthony Stevens about any of it! We can do whatever we want! If you want to stop, then we'll stop. We'll destroy Stevens and the book tonight if that's what you want. The important thing is that we're together now."

"Me and you?" she said. It could almost have made her laugh if she didn't know how utterly crazy he was.

He nodded. "I've wanted you a long time, Brooke. Since seventh grade, actually. But you were always so popular and I was ... well, *not*. I had to watch you hook up with guys like Todd who were so far beneath you it was a joke. But I wasn't laughing, Brooke! I knew I could treat you better than those guys ever could! And now I will! You'll see. You might not think much of me now, but I can show you. I can give you the life you deserve!"

"You're insane!" Brooke said.

His face turned thunderous. "Don't say that!" he snapped. "I did this for you, Brooke! I freed you from Todd!"

"Jesus Christ!" she said as she backed away from him.

"Where are you going, Brooke?" he demanded.

"Stay away from me!"

"Brooke!"

But she didn't want to hear it. She turned and ran. He pursued her, grabbing her by the shoulders. She turned around and brought her knee up, slamming it into his balls. He groaned and doubled over, sinking to the ground.

She didn't think to try and get the key off him. All she wanted to do was get away from him and his monstrous servant which must still be roaming the halls. She wanted to hide and headed for the nearest door.

It led into the auditorium and, as she flung it open and dashed through, she bumped straight into Lauren and Toby who were on their way out.

CHAPTER 15

"You're alive!" Brooke gasped.

"Yeah, it looks like Anthony Stevens recognizes me," said Lauren. "I guess he can't bring himself to kill his own daughter."

"Toby is insane!" Brooke said. "He set your father loose on Todd and Gary ... they're both dead! Jevicky never took the book, Toby still has it on him. It was all a lie to bring us here so he could kill Todd and Gary. And Toby has the key! We're locked in!"

Lauren's face paled at this. Being trapped in the school put paid to her plan of sneaking out with Corey through the side entrance they had come in through. Brooke pushed them back into the auditorium.

"We have to hide!" Brooke said.

"Wait, hide?" asked Lauren. "We need that key to get out! Where's Toby?"

"I don't know, I kneed him in the stones and then ran. Please, let's just hide in here!"

They closed the door to the auditorium and locked it. That left one other door on the far side and Corey hurried over to secure it. As he did so, somebody started rattling the first door on the other side. Both Lauren and Brooke screamed. Whoever was in the hallway beyond started hammering on the door, insistent on getting in.

"Up behind the stage," Lauren whispered to Brooke and Corey. "We can hide back there."

As the blows on the door increased in tempo and ferocity, they climbed up onto the stage and slipped behind the blue velvet curtain.

Several painted backdrops and screens hung there; half-finished set constructions for *A Midsummer Night's*

Dream. Lauren led them through the artificial woodland scenes to the crossover space and they squatted down in the shadows, hoping that the incessant banging on the doors would go away.

And it did, though the silence that followed it was almost as bad. Whoever had been banging on the door would be looking for another way in. Suddenly, the overhead lights flipped on. The three of them jumped as bright green light from the gels flooded their hiding place. It was like they had been plunged into a sunlit forest and they felt highly visible.

A door creaked somewhere, and Lauren froze, knowing that she had messed up. There was another entrance to the auditorium; a small door backstage that led to the technical room and then opened on the hallway behind the auditorium. She beckoned Corey and Brooke and they followed her behind one of the curtains, vanishing from view just as footsteps made the boards creak upstage.

Whoever was pursuing them was on the other side of the curtain and they tried to move as silently as they could to the other end without making the fabric rustle.

But they had run out of time. The curtain was jerked aside, and Toby thrust his crazed face through, a maniacal grin twisting his lips. "Well, looks like old Anthony isn't up to the job after all," he said. "I guess it's true what they say; if you want a job done well ... do it yourself!"

He held a long kitchen knife in his hand, apparently taken from the cafeteria. His plan was clear; to butcher the witnesses and make it look like Anthony Stevens had killed them.

"Run!" Lauren said, pushing Corey and Brooke ahead of her. They pelted across the stage as Toby's knife slashed viciously at Lauren's back, missing her by inches. Stumbling through the curtains, they made their way upstage towards the door to the technical room while Toby floundered and slashed about, hindered by the succession of curtains.

Next to the door to the technical room was a series of pulleys with which the curtains and backdrops were raised. Lauren grabbed one and quickly untangled it. The rope went whickering up and the backdrop hurtled down, landing on top of Toby, covering him like a cartoon ghost. He swore and slashed with his knife, cutting a slit in the painted fabric. By the time he was free, Lauren, Corey and Brooke had burst through the technical room and were in the hallway on the northern side of the school.

"We have to get out of here!" Brooke wailed.

"Not without the key, we can't!" said Lauren.

"Break a window or something!"

"They're all wire mesh glass!"

"Well, we have to think of something!"

There was a crash from the technical room as Toby stumbled into something. The three of them turned and ran, following the hallway but having no idea where to go. As they passed the stairs leading to the basement, Lauren turned and beckoned the others to follow her. There was no way out through the basement, but it was yet another hiding place and she just hoped that Toby wouldn't find them a second time.

They clattered down the stairs and entered the school's creepy underbelly filled with its boxes of junk and disused equipment and furniture. There were a ton of places to hide but Lauren preferably wanted a door to stand between them and the deranged Toby. The only place she could think of was the boiler room.

"This way!" she whispered to the others just as they heard Toby's footsteps in the stairwell. He had seen them go down into the basement and they didn't have much time.

The boiler room had a large iron door of the kind that wouldn't look out of place on a submarine. Lauren heaved it open, cursing its squeaky hinges, and held it while Corey and Brooke slipped in. Before she closed it behind her, she saw the shadow of Toby, thrown by the moonlight in the stairwell against the far wall. Biting her lip, she slowly shut the door and looked for a way to lock it.

There wasn't any.

Frantic now, she held onto the door handle and motioned Brooke to help find a way to secure it. Brooke's panicked eyes looked about the dim boiler room, lit a hellish orange by the maintenance light in its wire cage above them. There was a rickety old chair which the janitor parked his ass on occasionally, but the door opened outwards so they couldn't prop anything against it.

The door jerked in Lauren's hands, and she screamed as the handle almost slipped out of her grasp. "Help me!" she cried to Brooke as she tried to keep the door closed while Toby attempted to prize it open.

With both girls hauling on the handle, they were able to close the door, but Toby was stronger than he looked and with savage jerks, he kept yanking it open a few inches before they were able to slam it shut once more.

This futile tug of war continued for a couple of seconds while Corey ran and hid behind the gargantuan boiler. Lauren and Brooke sobbed as they realized that they were losing the battle and the door kept opening wider and wider until Toby was able to slide his knife blade in through the gap and slice it down towards their wrists.

They screamed and let go of the door just in time and Toby, knocked off balance as the door swung open, fell on his ass. The girls retreated into the shadows of the boiler room, edging around the humming machinery and hot pipes.

Toby got up, gave his knife a flourish. The orange light made it glimmer and cast his face in a demonic glow. He grinned, knowing that he had his prey trapped. As he entered the room, Lauren, Brooke and Corey tried to edge their way around the boiler, but he could see them through the wall of pipes and headed them off, forcing them into the back corner of the room.

"What do you want?" Brooke wailed.

"I just want you, darling," Toby purred. "And I want to kill those two snoops back there with you. We can't let them live, Brooke, you can see that right? Why don't you just come out of there and help me finish them off?"

"Fuck you!" Brooke yelled. "You're fucking crazy!"

"Aw, come on, Brooke! Why are you defending them? You didn't care about my stepdad or about Mrs. Ross. And I thought you hated that Lauren bitch, anyway? She's *his* daughter for fuck's sake!"

"I didn't want to kill anybody!" said Brooke. "That was all you and Todd."

"Right, but you didn't exactly try to stop us either, huh? Now you're getting on your high horse over Lauren fucking Stevens?"

"That's not my name!" Lauren yelled, stepping out from behind the pipes.

Toby lunged with his knife. She ducked back behind cover and the edge of the blade slid across the flaky paint of the pipes. He stabbed again, this time in between the pipes and nearly skewered Lauren's shoulder.

"Stop it!" Brooke howled.

Lauren's back was pressed up against the wall as Toby tried to reach her with his knife, his whole forearm squeezed between the pipes. He was unaware of the shadow that had entered the room behind him. Lauren saw it and so did Brooke and Corey.

It was Anthony Stevens, standing right behind Toby, his master. Lauren saw that same struggle in his rotten features that she had seen when he hadn't been able to kill her. He was battling something deep within and he apparently won for he grabbed Toby's head in both hands and wrenched him away from Lauren.

Confusion spread across Toby's features, and he spun around to face Anthony. His eyes widened in terror at his own creation now turned on him and he jammed the kitchen knife into Anthony's chest. It had no effect. Anthony Stevens no longer felt pain and Lauren doubted he could be killed by any conventional means.

Toby looked down at the knife, embedded up to the hilt in the man's chest. Anthony grabbed his head with his hands once more and began to squeeze. As he slid his thumbs into Toby's eye sockets, Lauren, Brooke and Corey made their escape from the boiler room, slipping around the side of the boiler and running out the door just as Toby's high-pitched wailing filled the basement, accompanied by a sickening wet crunching sound.

They bolted for the stairs and didn't stop running until they were around the corner of the hallway above.

"Wait!" Laura panted. "We still can't get out! We need the keys!"

"Fuck the keys!" Brooke cried. "There has to be another way out of here!"

"No! We have to go back!"

"Are you crazy? We can't go back there! That thing will kill us!"

"Not me," Lauren said, shaking her head.

"Yeah, she's right," Corey said. "Anthony Stevens is her father. He won't touch her. In fact, he just saved her life."

"Stay with Corey," Lauren instructed Brooke. "I'm going back."

"No, don't leave us!" Brooke whimpered. "Please!"

"It'll be OK," Lauren told her. Brooke was terrified out of her wits and was practically pawing at her to make her stay. "I'll only be gone a moment and then we can get out of here. Brooke, listen to me! You have to take care of Corey!"

"Yeah," said Corey, cottoning on to what Lauren was doing and playing his part admirably, though she didn't know how frightened he might actually be. "You have to stay with me, Brooke. I'm scared."

Brooke looked from Lauren to Corey, unsure.

"I'll be right back," Lauren said.

She turned and left them before Brooke had a chance to protest and made her way back towards the stairs that led down into the basement. Her heart was pounding at the thought of going back down into that dingy boiler room, seeing Toby's mangled corpse and confronting the specter of her father but she just had to do it. It was their only way out of the school. She had to do it for Corey.

The orange light from the boiler room spilled across the basement, stretching the shadows devilishly long and thin. Trying not to make a sound, Lauren crept around the shelves and piles of junk, keeping her eyes and ears open for any sign of her father. What if he had taken Toby's body away? What then?

But Toby was right where they had left him, sprawled on the boiler room floor, his head horribly crushed, and his eyeballs pulped so the blood and jelly ran from the sockets. Fighting down the nausea rising in her throat, Lauren crept towards the body and knelt down by its side.

First, she checked the jeans pockets. The key to the side door was in his right pocket and she had to squeeze her hand in there to wiggle it out. Then she checked his denim jacket for the book he had pretended to lose. Brooke had said that he had it on him and there it was, in the inside pocket. It was such a tatty old school notebook. How could such an unassuming piece of crap hold the power over life and death, the power to summon the dead and command them to kill?

She shoved the book into the pocket of her own jacket and stood up, gripping the key in her right hand. Hurrying from the hellish room and the stink of death, she made her way back towards the stairs.

In the tail of her eye, she saw a shape rise from the gloom. It was *him*. He had been lurking down here, perhaps even watching her. She found herself frozen to the spot, unable to cross the last few yards and reach the stairs.

He shambled closer and a strange noise emanated from his rotten vocal cords. It began as a whispery moan as of a coma patient who hasn't spoken in months. By the light from the boiler room, she could see his shriveled lips undulating like worms as they tried to turn the moan into speech.

"Lllaurennn ..." he mumbled.

The sound of her name from those decayed lips sent a shiver down to her very core. There was no doubt about it now; he remembered her and what's more ... he wanted to *talk* to her.

It was too much for Lauren and she turned and ran for the stairs, tears stinging her eyes. Why couldn't he have stayed dead? Why did Toby and the others have to drag the past back to life? Would she never be free of that man and his awful crimes?

She took the stairs two at a time and made her way down the hallway to where Brooke and Corey were waiting for her.

"You got it?" Brooke asked

"Yeah," Lauren replied, wiping away her tears with the sleeve of her sweater. "And I also got this." She pulled the notebook from her pocket and showed them. "Now, let's get out of here and find a way to kill that monster."

They hurried down to the gymnasium, looking over their shoulders every so often to make sure they weren't being pursued. Something had obviously happened in the gymnasium as there were several javelins scattered about and Lauren briefly wondered what sort of end Gary had come to.

She tried to push the thought from her mind as they ran towards the side door. A twist of the key and they were out and running across the darkened parking lot towards the Lipstadt's station wagon. Todd's beloved van was parked not far over, never to be driven by its owner again. Lauren fumbled for the keys and got in behind the wheel of the station wagon while Brooke got in beside her and Corey dove into the back. Brooke screamed and pointed through the windshield at the figure of Anthony Stevens emerging from the gymnasium.

"Get out of here, Lauren!" Corey yelled from the back seat.

Anthony broke into a run as Lauren turned the key in the ignition and revved the engine. Apparently, the dead could move fast if they wanted to, and Antony cleared the distance across the asphalt in enough time to jump and land on the hood of the car as Lauren spun the wheel and nosed it in the direction of the school gates.

Brooke screamed again. The rotten face of Anthony Stevens leered in at them through the windshield, blocking Lauren's view of the parking lot ahead. Jerking the wheel this way and that, she succeeded in making

Anthony roll from side to side until he lost his purchase on the car and slid off.

The tires squealed on the asphalt as Lauren accelerated and a glance in the rear-view mirror showed that Anthony was left behind them in the parking lot, watching them leave.

CHAPTER 16

Lauren drove straight back to Corey's house. There wasn't even any talk of dropping Brooke off at her own house. They were all in this now and each of them wanted to see it through to the end, whatever end that may be. It was strange for Lauren to be doing anything with the bully who had made her life miserable for the past five years, but she knew Brooke was terrified out of her wits and found herself even taking pity on her. She swore to herself that her father had claimed his last victim this night.

As she parked up, she glanced down the street and saw the darkened windows of the Lipstadt's house. They were all fast asleep, like most of the town, oblivious to the awful things that had gone on up at the high school. Lauren just hoped that Mr. and Mrs. Lipstadt and Harriet wouldn't be awoken by the car engine or closing of its doors. They needed time to try and undo the evil the book in her pocket had summoned.

Once inside Corey's house, the three of them examined the book around the dining table. To be reading the translated words of a satanic medieval priest felt deeply weird to Lauren. Corey was all over it, of course, reading passages aloud with glee like it was all some sort of game. She hadn't the heart to tell him it was way past his bedtime. Normal things like bedtimes and responsibly looking after a child had gone out the window hours ago.

"This is all very cryptic," said Lauren in exasperation once they had read through the notebook from cover to cover. "It talks about manifesting the spirits of the dead in corporeal form and controlling them, but how did you guys know who you were bringing back?"

"We weren't actually trying to bring back Anthony Stevens," said Brooke. "We wanted to bring back the people your father ... um, *Anthony Stevens* killed. We each sacrificed a talisman belonging to a loved one he killed. I burned a teddy keychain that was my sister's ... We were trying to bring them back, to undo what he had done. Somehow it all went horribly wrong and, well, we just kind of went with it."

"But there's nothing about sacrifices in the book," said Lauren. "It just says what words to say. How did you know how to do the actual ritual?"

"That was all Toby," said Brooke. "He was the occult nut. We figured he understood this stuff and knew what to do. I guess he mixed the incantations from this book with his own brand of black magic and the wrong spirit came back. We don't even know what that phrase in the ancient language even says. Jesus, we were so dumb!"

She flopped down on the nearby sofa and buried her head in her hands.

"This bit about controlling a revenant," said Lauren. "That was what Toby used once you guys figured that Anthony Stevens wouldn't hurt you. That he was your revenant to control, right?"

"Yeah. Then I guess he figured out how to turn him on Todd and Gary. He has a little altar to Satan in his bedroom. The guy was real freaky. None of us liked him very much."

"But there's nothing here about what to do when you no longer require the revenant!" said Lauren desperately.

"Guess it would have been a good idea to try and keep Toby alive," said Corey. "He's the only one who knew anything about all this. But even he only got it half right, I guess."

"Well, that's just great!" said Lauren slapping the notebook closed. "This book of spells is just a load of mumbo-jumbo if it doesn't tell us exactly what we need to do!"

"Well, there's always the more traditional way of dispatching zombies," said Corey. The two girls looked at him. "You know, burning, dismemberment. The old stake through the heart, though that's mostly vampires, I guess. I wonder if he'd still be able to walk about after being beheaded? Lore says that you can kill a vampire by beheading it but not always a zombie."

"Where are you getting all that stuff?" Brooke asked from the sofa.

He turned and shrugged at her. "Horror movies."

"It'll work just as well, I guess," said Lauren. "I mean, he can't exactly hurt anybody if we chop him up into tiny bits or burn him to a crisp."

"Let's burn him," said Brooke. "I don't exactly have the stomach for chopping somebody up into little bits, even Anthony Stevens."

"Agreed," said Lauren. "And I'd rather there wasn't a single scrap of him left in existence. Just dust in the wind, blowing far away from here would suit me just fine."

The phrase 'dust in the wind' made her think of that Kansas song her mother used to play all the time. It was one of mom's favorites and she choked back a rising sob. There was no time to get emotional. They had a monster to kill.

"Just one problem, ladies," said Corey. "How the hell do we find him? We left him in the school parking lot. He could be anywhere in Crimson Bay right about now, stalking old ladies or terrorizing their dogs."

"He doesn't just kill at random," said Lauren. "He has to be commanded to kill, right Brooke?"

"Well, yeah ..." said Brooke uncertainly.

"By the way, did you command him to kill that couple in the camper van up on Mount Lenzi or was that some other sicko? Jesus, I hope there's just the one in town."

"We didn't have anything to do with that," said Brooke. "But it happened the night we did the summoning, as Toby called it. I guess Anthony Stevens just came across those campers. Maybe they threatened him. The first time we saw Anthony, we all threw rocks and stuff at him, and he didn't do anything because we controlled him. But he went for Todd when Todd attacked him. Todd never made the sacrifice, at least that's what Toby said. He never lost anybody five years ago, so he didn't burn a talisman to summon the dead."

"OK, so we know that he only kills people who get in his way," said Corey. "Still not good news. And we have no idea where to look for him."

"Yes, we do," said Lauren. They both looked at her. "You said that Anthony sticks mostly to the woods surrounding Mount Lenzi, right?"

Brooke nodded.

"Well, he must have some place to hide when he's not out murdering people. What better place than those woods? And he even has a house there."

"The old Stevens house?" Brooke said. "Is that place still standing?"

"It was five years ago," said Lauren, shivering a little at the memory of being dragged to that old house in the woods by her father back when he had been a living, breathing man. If he still remembered her, then surely he still remembered his old house.

"It must be a ruin by now," said Brooke. "Nobody's lived there since Mrs. Stevens died years ago."

"Well, zombies aren't exactly picky about housing standards," said Corey. "Lauren's right, that's gotta be where he's hiding out in the daytime."

"Then we go there tonight," said Lauren. "And burn that fucker!"

"Hell, yeah!" said Corey, pumping the air with his fist. "Hey, you know what's best for toasting somebody from a distance?"

"Flamethrower?" Brooke volunteered.

"I like your thinking but I'm not sure we have the materials for one of those. We do have a buttload of coke bottles in the basement along with a can of gasoline and some old rags. You ladies ever heard of a Molotov cocktail?"

"Jesus, you're a weird kid," said Brooke.

"You got any better ideas?" he asked, a little affronted.

"All right, it's a good idea," said Lauren. "Show us what to do, Corey."

Beaming, Corey led them down to the basement and flipped on the light switch. He dragged a yellow plastic case of glass coke bottles out from under and table and then went into the garage in search of gasoline.

Lauren was pretty sure making Molotov cocktails wasn't in *The Complete Babysitter's Handbook*, but what was one more bad decision in a whole night of bad decisions? The three of them stood at the table and got to work; Lauren and Brooke pouring gasoline into the bottles while Corey tore up strips of rags to use as fuses.

"Hey, Lauren?" said Brooke when Corey ran out of rags and went upstairs to grab hand towels and dishcloths.

"Yeah?"

"I'm sorry. You know, for being such a bitch for the past few years?"

Lauren blinked, not really knowing what to say. This whole night had been like one weird dream where everything was turned on its head. If somebody had said to her earlier that day that she would be making Molotov cocktails with Brooke McKenna and that Brooke McKenna was actually apologizing for being a bully, she would have told them that they were crazy.

"It's fine ... I guess," she said. "I know life hasn't exactly been easy for you after ... you know, losing your sister."

"It's not just losing her," said Brooke as she held another bottle steady for Lauren to pour gasoline into. "It's how my parents reacted to the whole thing. I mean, I get it, your favorite daughter got murdered, you're bound to be depressed, but it's like they totally forgot I existed. I miss her too but there was never anybody to talk to about her. Any time I mentioned Jill's name I got yelled at for making them sad all over again so eventually I just stopped trying to think about her. I guess I took it out on you a little because you were his daughter. But I never really thought about you losing your parents that night which must have been even worse."

"Anthony Stevens – *my father* – took so much from everybody in Crimson Bay," said Lauren. "It's like the whole town has been in grief for the past five years. I guess nobody wanted to even look at me because I just reminded them ..."

"Yeah. Well, that was wrong and I'm sorry. All we tried to do was bring back our loved ones and instead we brought back the very thing that took them from us. If Toby was still alive, I'd kill him all over again."

"Let's just focus on killing Anthony Stevens, huh?" Lauren asked with a smile.

Brooke smiled back. "Deal."

Corey returned with some of his mom's hand towels and began ripping them into strips. There was going to be so much explaining to do once all this was over, but

Lauren guessed that a few missing hand towels were going to be the least of their problems.

When they were finished, they had a dozen or so Molotov cocktails, each with a gasoline-soaked rag poking out of the top like rats' tails. They gently slid each bottle back into the plastic crate to stop them rattling around and potentially breaking during transit.

"Do you have anything to eat in the house?" Brooke asked Corey. "I'm starved."

"PB&J sandwiches?" Corey offered.

"Fine."

Lauren found that she was hungry too. It had been several hours since dinner and they had all burned a lot of energy. It was decided that food was an important prerequisite to taking the fight to Anthony up in those woods, so they decamped to the kitchen and fixed a late-night feast. While Brooke and Corey smeared peanut butter and jelly on slices of Wonder Bread, Lauren carried the first crate of Molotovs out to the trunk of the station wagon.

As she deposited the crate, she closed the trunk as softly as she could so as not to wake any neighbors and, as she rounded the car, she spotted old Mrs. Wallace in her back yard, floral nightie billowing in the wind.

Oh, great, she thought. That's just what tonight needed. Mrs. Wallace having another episode. Did she often walk about at night or was this just the worst timing in the world? Either way, they couldn't afford any kind of scene waking up the neighbors. Not tonight, of all nights.

She decided to try and get the old coot back indoors like before. "Mrs. Wallace?" she whispered as she approached. "Are you alright?"

"Night has come, night has come, all flown away," the old lady replied.

"Would you like me to help you back inside?"

Mrs. Wallace smiled as Lauren entered her backyard and gently steered her towards her house. "You've seen him?" Mrs. Wallace said. "You've seen that poor boy?"

"Let's just get you indoors," said Lauren. "You'll catch your death out here."

The wind was chill, and Mrs. Wallace had only a thin nightie cloaking her frail frame. She belonged in a home, not left to fend for herself, Lauren thought angrily.

None of the lights were on in the house and she fumbled for the kitchen light switch as she closed the door behind them. She led Mrs. Wallace to her armchair in the living room and helped her into it before fetching her a blanket.

"Oh, I'm so sorry," said the old lady, seeming to snap out of the daze she had been in moments previously. "I get so confused sometimes. It's my medicine ... I don't always remember to take it and it doesn't always work in any case ..."

"That's quite all right, Mrs. Wallace," said Lauren, fetching a tartan blanket from the arm of the sofa. "Your daughter explained everything."

"You helped me before, and I'm so grateful," Mrs. Wallace said. "Such a nice girl. Just like your mother."

That froze Lauren for a heartbeat. She should just let it go and get back to Brooke and Corey. They had too much to do tonight to allow herself to get sidetracked but, having learned that Mrs. Wallace had once been a teacher at Crimson Bay High and that she had known her parents as well as Anthony Stevens, curiosity got the better of her. "You used to teach up at the high school, didn't you Mrs. Wallace."

The old lady smiled. "Oh, yes. Thirty-four years. It's changed quite a bit now, I suppose."

"And you knew my parents? Ronette Shaye and Jeff Mackenzie?"

At this, the wistful smile on the old lady's face withered to a frown. "Yes ... I knew them both. Ronette was lovely. Always willing to help, always nice to those who needed it. Especially to that poor Stevens boy."

"*Anthony* Stevens?" Lauren asked, sure that she was talking about some other Stevens kid.

"Yes, poor Anthony Stevens. He had a horrible time fitting in. The other kids used to tease him something awful. It was on account of being the only kid with a single mom. It was different in those days, you see, and the fact that they lived way out in the woods, away from everybody else didn't help. It made him a bit of an odd child. People thought he was a bit spooky, I guess, but he was a nice boy, at least to begin with."

Lauren had no idea what to say to that. Didn't she know what Anthony Stevens had done? What he became? Perhaps it was the senility that was causing her to misremember things or just plain forget.

But the old lady wasn't finished talking.

"He was so desperately in love with your mother, Lauren," she said. "I think it was because she was the only one who had a kind word for him. That was just how she was. When she saw somebody hurting, she just wanted to help. They became friends. *More* than friends. Of course, all the other kids made a big fuss about it, but your mother didn't seem to care. Good to the very core of her soul, she was, and I had never seen Anthony look so happy.

"But Jeff Mackenzie, now, he was bad news, and I don't like to speak ill of the dead but there it is. He was crazy about your mother. They had dated a little and I guess he felt like he owned her or something and it just about drove him over the edge to see her with Anthony. He was one of the worst of the bullies, I'm afraid, and people said that she did it just to spite him, but I don't believe that. Ronette Shaye wouldn't use somebody like that. She didn't have a mean bone in her body, but Jeff sure did, and he made sure to fix things for Anthony for good.

"It was Jeff who started the rumor, you see. Two little girls had been assaulted down by the river. They had wandered off from where their parents were having a picnic and said that a man had come and done horrible things to them. The police were looking high and low for this man and your father handed over Anthony Stevens as the perfect suspect. He said that he'd seen Anthony in the area as he was driving through, not half an hour before the girls were molested. That was about all anybody needed to see him as guilty. He was such an odd boy, you see, and Jeff Mackenzie, well, he was quite popular. Came from the right family with a lot of connections. Anthony didn't stand a chance and, from what I heard, the questioning methods used on those two girls were extremely suggestive. A child psychologist from another state kicked up a huge stink at the trial, claiming that they had been coerced to the point of having 'false memories'. Well, nobody around here wanted to hear much about that, so it was more or less an open and shut case."

"Wait a minute," Lauren said, feeling a little breathless. "Are you saying the allegations against Anthony Stevens weren't true?"

"None of it was true. It was all lies cooked up by your father and a town looking for a scapegoat. Whoever that man was who molested those girls, it wasn't Anthony Stevens. One of them recanted her testimony a couple of years later but by then it was too late. Poor Anthony was locked up with the worst people in the country and the things they did to him in there ... I don't like to dwell on it."

Lauren swallowed heavily.

"They turned him into a monster," Mrs. Wallace continued. "When he escaped, well, he wasn't the same boy who went in there fourteen years before. Fourteen years in that place! It was no wonder he was looking for revenge, not that I can condone what he did. But this town had its reckoning, no doubt about it."

"I ... uh, I need to get back," said Lauren. Her whole body felt numb, and she desperately needed some fresh air.

"You head home now, Lauren," Mrs. Wallace said. "And thank you for your help again. I'll be all right here. Go on, now."

As Lauren headed towards the back door, she turned to look at Mrs. Wallace in her chair, knowing that she had to tell her. "Anthony Stevens ..." she said. "You know that he's ... he's my real father?"

Mrs. Wallace smiled. "Oh, I know that, dear. We all knew. Your mother was already showing before Anthony went on trial. It broke her heart. But don't let it upset you. The past is past."

CHAPTER 17

Lauren took deep gulps of the cool night air and tried to calm her jumping nerves. The story Mrs. Wallace had told her had turned everything around in her head and made it all a horrible jumble. She was half tempted to try and ignore the old woman's words and put it all down to her faulty memory and senility, but she knew that wouldn't be honest. There was too much about what she had said that rang true. And deep down, she knew it *was* true, all of it.

Her father had been innocent.

That didn't excuse the killing spree he had embarked on after breaking out of prison five years ago, but it did make her see Anthony Stevens in a whole new light. He hadn't always been a monster. Like her, he had been a quiet, shy kid who didn't fit in and had fallen victim to the cruelties of small-town gossip and prejudice. And he hadn't been a child molester. His crimes had started *after* he had been sent to prison.

She was still angry at him. How could she not be? He had murdered so many innocent people for the sins of others and, in so doing, had ruined her life. She had grown up in a town that had hated her from her very birth because of him. He had even murdered her mother so she never got the chance to ask her about him or find out the truth. Instead, she had to learn the truth from a half-crazed old neighbor who seemed to be the only person in this damned town who wasn't afraid to talk about the past.

She might be angry at Anthony Stevens – that was a given – but she had a newfound anger for Crimson Bay, all of it, from its teachers to its parents to its cops. They had all known and they had all played their part. Pinning the blame on Anthony Stevens had been easy.

Lazy. *Evil.* And it had been their own children who had suffered for it. How many of those victims who had died up on that mountain that night had parents who had stood by and let her father go to jail back in 1968, knowing deep down that he was innocent? Prison had stripped every shred of humanity from him so that he emerged the monster this town had made him.

It was all a horrible, vicious circle. The crimes of the past haunted the children of the future. How many more people had to suffer for the stupid and callous actions of a past generation? The anger inside her swelled to a point where she felt like she must burst. It had to end tonight, on that she was decided. And she also decided that nobody else would get hurt. Not Corey and not Brooke. This was her fight. Her family. She wouldn't drag them into this more than they had been already.

That meant she had to do this alone.

She went back to the car, opened the driver's seat and got in, closing it softly behind her. She had a set of wheels, a crate of Molotov cocktails in the trunk and a lighter in her pocket. And she had the determination to see the job done.

Turning the key in the ignition, she rolled away from the sidewalk and headed down the street, turning left at the end, in the direction of the large, black hump of Mount Lenzi.

"Did you hear that?" asked Corey around a mouthful of PB&J sandwich.

"Hear what?" asked Brooke, her head in the refrigerator as she looked for the milk.

"It sounded like a car starting up."

"So?"

"So, it's a quiet street. Most people are asleep."

He got out from behind the kitchen table and headed into the living room. Peering through the blinds, he let out a curse that even Brooke felt like chiding him for.

"She's gone! She took the car and left!"

"Who, Lauren?"

"No. Nancy Reagan! Who do you think!"

"What the hell is she doing, leaving us? Isn't she supposed to be babysitting you?"

"Oh, shit!" Corey exclaimed. "She's going at it alone! She's gonna take him on by herself!"

"Why?"

"Because it's some father-daughter thing, I guess. She's gonna get massacred! Hey, we need to go after her."

"How? She took the car."

"We have my mom's."

"Isn't she at work?"

"Yeah, but she carpools with somebody. Come on, let's get going! You grab the other case of Molotovs and I'll grab the keys!"

Cursing under her breath at this new curveball the night had thrown at her, Brooke did as he asked, and they headed down into the garage where a dark blue 1981 Audi was parked.

They stowed the Molotovs in the trunk and got in, Corey yanking the cord that raised the rolling door as he did so. Brooke started up the engine and the car shot forward with a jolt.

"Hey, watch the Molotovs!" Corey cried.

"Sorry!" said Brooke. She eased the car out of the garage and turned up the street with several jolts.

"You can actually drive, right?" Corey asked, glancing at her sidelong.

"Well, my dad gave me some lessons," Brooke replied, her eyes alternating between the gear shifter and the street ahead. "But that was some time ago."

"You mean you don't have your license? Aw, man!"

"We'll be fine," said Brooke with a confidence that Corey saw through entirely. "After all, it's not like we haven't broken a bunch of laws already tonight, is it?"

The darkness of the woods seemed to claw at Lauren as she headed up the dirt track towards the old Stevens house. The headlights made a white, spiny tunnel of the road ahead and she couldn't escape the feeling that she was being swallowed down some dark throat.

The house was there, at the end of the track, more or less as she remembered it. A little more rundown perhaps, and more overgrown, as if the woods were trying to reclaim the land and erase the infection of evil.

She parked out front, switched off the engine and gazed at those black windows for a while, not sure if she had the guts to do what she needed to do after all. That house, with its flaky, peeling boards streaked with graffiti and gaping, sad windows had haunted her dreams for the past five years. She had a vague impression of its interior with its peeling wallpaper and sense of abandonment, but it was like something from a dream, no a *nightmare*.

It was within those rotten walls that she had seen her mother's corpse, sitting at the dinner table, her throat slashed from ear to ear, posed liked some ghastly puppet in a demented show. Her father had just wanted the three of them to be together again and all Lauren had wanted to do was to scream.

He was insane, there had never been any doubt about that, and Lauren knew that she had to summon the courage to finish this, no matter what was waiting for her inside that house of horrors.

She got out, fetched the crate of Molotovs from the trunk and approached the house. She guessed that her father would still be making his way back to his lair from the high school, so she intended to lie in wait for him.

The front door was open and, as soon as she set foot in that dim hallway, memories of her previous night there swarmed her mind. She fought them like demons, pushing them out of her consciousness so she could focus on the task at hand.

The place didn't look like anybody had been living there, but then, she guessed nobody had. Her father was as dead as a doornail. What signs of life would he leave? It wasn't as if he ate anything. She wondered if he even slept or if he just stood in an empty room and waited to be called upon to murder.

She shuddered at the thought and glanced from room to room to make sure she really was alone, before depositing the crate of Molotovs on the dining table, trying not to think of the last time she had seen that table.

She was fairly confident that she was alone in the house. After all, it would take him some time to shamble through the suburbs and up into the woods. She dreaded to think of somebody coming across his path. From what Brooke had said, that was the only reason he would kill, and she dearly hoped that Toby had been her father's last victim.

But she didn't feel quite safe enough waiting inside the house for his return without checking the upstairs bedrooms. Steeling her nerves, she headed up the stairs, hating the way the old wood creaked and groaned under her weight.

The Stevens house had only two bedrooms and a ruin of a bathroom where fungi sprouted through the broken tiles. The larger of the two rooms had once been a soft pink but now green and black spots of mold grew on the wallpaper and the large double bed was thick with dust. A dresser with a cracked mirror and all of its drawers missing sat in the corner and Lauren realized that this had been the bedroom of Mrs. Stevens, the grandmother she had never met.

The other bedroom had trains on the wallpaper and nothing else in it but dust and dead flies. This was her father's bedroom and the only one he had ever known except for a jail cell.

There was the sound of rustling bushes through the broken windowpane and Lauren crept over to it and looked out into the overgrown yard below. A long shadow of somebody passing around the corner of the building was cast on the dirt by the light of the moon and Lauren felt her heartbeat quicken.

He had returned.

She crept out of the bedroom and waited on the landing for him to come thundering in through the front door. She hadn't much of a plan other than confronting him and hoping that his reluctance to kill her would hold out. Somehow, she had to get close enough to hurl a Molotov at him but not so close that he might stop her or that she might be engulfed in the ensuing inferno.

She waited but he didn't come in.

Was he still lurking outside? What for?

Then it occurred to her that he had seen the car. He might not recognize it from the school parking lot, so he wouldn't know it was her who had come all the way out here. She cursed herself for not hiding it from view. He was probably freaked out by a late-night visitor, or as freaked out as a semi-sentient zombie could be.

She crept down the stairs, her eyes on the front door, her body tense. The night beyond the walls of the house was silent and she wished that she could hear him moving about out there. She hated not knowing where he was or what he was doing.

She entered the hallway and then backed slowly away from the front door, towards the dining room and the crate of Molotovs, her fingers reaching into her pocket for her lighter. Once he entered the house, she intended to light him up like a Roman candle. She fumbled for the lighter and, just as she withdrew it, the back door burst open, and a figure lunged into the kitchen.

She spun around, a cry of terror on her lips as her father lumbered through the house towards her, gnarled hands outstretched as if he meant to crush her to death with his bare hands. The sound of her voice halted him in his tracks and, once again, he recognized his daughter.

He stood dumbly before her, mouth twisting around words that wouldn't come. She held the lighter in her hand, equally impotent with nothing to light and the two of them stared at each other, neither quite knowing what to do.

Lauren wondered if she should push her luck and try and move into the dining room. If she could reach the crate of Molotovs without him knowing what she was up to, then she had a chance. But fear froze her in position. Fear of what he might do if she made either a sudden run for it, or if she backed away slowly. Indecision paralyzed her.

And then, he started to move towards her, rotten boots sliding across the grimy vinyl of the kitchen floor. She slowly backed away from him, shrinking from those awful hands which had committed such atrocities. What was he doing? Trying to *hug* her?

The thought made her stomach churn. She was at the threshold of the dining room now and decided that this was close enough. She turned and ran into the room, but he was quicker than she credited him. Vice-like arms seized her around the middle. The lighter flew from her grasp and skittered across the dusty floorboards.

She fought against him, but he had her and he was so strong! Turning her around, he gazed on her face with those black, depthless eye sockets and then crushed her to him. She choked on a sob and tried to block out the stink of his rotten rags and flesh as he squeezed her to his chest, embracing his long-lost daughter.

CHAPTER 18

"We're lost, aren't we?" Corey asked as Brooke turned down yet another tree-lined avenue.

"Not lost, exactly," said Brooke. "I'm sure one of these streets leads to the highway. I wish I'd paid more attention when Todd was driving!"

"You and me both," Corey grumbled.

"Shut it, you little pipsqueak!" Brooke snapped. "I'm *not* lost!"

A car turned the corner up ahead and came towards them. It had a dark body with a black top.

"Uh, isn't that ... a cop car?" Corey said.

"Shit!" Brooke exclaimed. "It's Sheriff Weiss! Oh, I hope he doesn't want to ask us what we're doing driving around at night!"

"With no license," Corey added.

"Just put your head down," said Brooke. "He might not think twice if he doesn't see a kid out cruising at night."

"Hey, it's *my* mom's car!"

"Do what I say, you little jerk!"

Brooke grabbed Corey's shaggy mop of hair and shoved him down in his seat so he wouldn't be visible over the dashboard just as the police cruiser glided past. She tried not to make eye contact with Sheriff Weiss as they passed each other but felt his stare on her all the same.

"Did we make it?" Corey's muffled voice said down by the footwell.

"I think so," said Brooke, glancing in the rearview mirror.

Sheriff Weiss wheeled around to tail them, and the red and blue light flashed atop his cruiser.

"Shit!" said Brooke. "What do we do now?"

"If we stop, he'll haul us in and then we'll never save Lauren!" said Corey. "Just hit it!"

Without thinking, Brooke did what he suggested and floored the gas pedal. The wheels spun in a squeal of rubber and the car shot forward.

What am I doing? she thought to herself miserably. *A car chase on top of everything else? I am so dead!*

But the consequences of being picked up with no license, not to mention having to explain everything to Sheriff Weiss made her more determined to outrun her pursuer. She gave the steering wheel a hard jerk to the left and they cut across the road and rumbled onto the scrubby ground of a vacant lot.

"What the hell are you doing?" Corey yelled as they bounced around inside the car.

"I'm pretty sure this lot leads to that stretch of crappy land behind the old park," Brooke said. "We can throw him off our tail that way."

"Whatever you say, Bo Duke!"

The ground sloped down to the wooded glen that served as the border between the Crimson Bay suburbs and the forest that clung to the feet of Mount Lenzi and it sloped a little deeper than Brooke had anticipated. They were both flung forward as the car lurched downwards and then all was branches and foliage whipping at the windshield.

"I can't see!" Brooke wailed as she gripped the steering wheel with white-knuckled hands.

Corey yelled in terror as the left wheel bounced off a stubborn root and the car jolted sickeningly as they continued their descent. Brooke screamed as she wrestled with the car, narrowly avoiding a tree trunk.

Eventually, the trees thinned a little as the edge of the park came into view. Brooke jerked the steering wheel this way and that to avoid refrigerators and rusted boilers and other bits of junk.

"Keep going!" Corey yelled, looking behind them at Sheriff Weiss who had followed them down the slope and was doing a fair job of keeping on their tail, siren wailing every step of the way.

"There's the highway up ahead!" Brooke said.

The ground sloped up to the road which was bordered by a white fence.

"Hit it, Chewie!" Corey yelled. "He's gaining on us!"

Once again, Brooke floored the gas and they rocketed towards the slope. "We're not gonna make it!" she cried as the tires slithered on the grass.

"Yes we are!" Corey said. "Don't let up!"

She didn't and they both let out a howl of terror as the car crested the ridge and burst through the white picket fence, slithering across the blacktop wildly until Brooke was able to get it under control and bring it to a shuddering stop, stalling it in the process.

They peered out her window at Sheriff Weiss's cruiser which had sidewinded a tree and come to a standstill, its siren and lights still lighting up the glen.

"We did it!" Corey said, holding his hand up for a high-five.

Her own hand shaking, Brooke slapped his and then returned her grip to the steering wheel.

"Well, we found the highway at last," said Corey. "You know the way now?"

Brooke gave him a withering look before she turned the ignition and, in a squeal of rubber, they were off.

Sheriff Weiss flipped off the siren. He sat for a moment staring through his windshield at the dense foliage around him in disbelief. He'd been outmaneuvered, and by a kid at that.

He hadn't caught much of a glimpse of the girl behind the wheel, but the blonde frizzy hair in a side ponytail was a dead ringer for Brooke McKenna. He'd cautioned that punk, Todd Cates enough times to recognize his gum-chewing girlfriend in the passenger seat of his van, but he'd never seen her out driving on her own before. And what she was doing driving a family car at a quarter to eleven on a Friday night was anyone's guess.

Damn kid had probably stolen it, but then where was Todd or any of those other goons she hung around with? Toby Johnson was one of them. No sign of him tonight but Sheriff Weiss got a feeling deep in his gut that something bad was happening. He didn't know how he knew it, he just *knew*.

He picked up the CB radio and put out an APB on the blue Audi. Then he requested a tow truck be sent to drag him out of this mess. Goddamn, but this was embarrassing!

Lauren fought down the urge to sob as her father wheeled her around and around the dining room like some depraved puppeteer. He was actually *dancing* with her, ballroom style or the closest thing the memory of Anthony Stevens had of the concept.

They had been doing this for some time and Lauren felt desperately tired. Her father, clearly thrilled that his long-lost daughter had wandered into his own house, had wasted no time in getting reacquainted. Round and round they went, to no music but that which played inside his cracked skull, his clumsy, booted feet thudding on the floorboards and occasionally landing on her sore and bruised toes.

How would this end? He clearly wanted to play happy families but what would he try once the dancing had stopped? Visons of father-daughter activities given a grotesque makeover flashed through Lauren's mind and she truly felt like she was going mad. Her initial plan had failed, and she was now the prisoner in some awful and perverted game.

The headlights of a car swept the room and her father suddenly stopped dancing, his head snapping to look out the front window. The sound of a car stalling could be heard and the headlights winked out.

Somebody was out there!

Lauren prayed that it was the cops; Sheriff Weiss come to rescue her a second time. And this time, he had better finish the job.

Voices. A girl and a young boy trying to be quiet as they approached the house. Lauren's heart sank. It was Brooke and Corey, come to rescue her.

"Get away!" she yelled to them. "Get ou ..."

Her father's hand clamped over her mouth, the disgusting, cold and worm-eaten fingers pressing against her lips. He was in a panic at the sudden arrival of strangers and began dragging Lauren into the hallway.

She kicked and flailed but he was too strong, and she became aware of him opening a door under the stairs that led down to some sort of cellar. Fresh fear coursed through her as he half shoved, half dragged her down the wooden steps which led into utter blackness. Screaming, she tried to get past him, but his tall frame filled the narrow stairway and, turning and striding up the steps, he slammed the door shut and slid the bolt home.

Still screaming, Lauren hammered on the door, the damp, clammy blackness of the cellar all around her. Unfortunately, the door was about the only sturdy thing left in the house and, try as she might, she couldn't budge it.

"Corey! Brooke!" she yelled as she heard her father's footsteps recede down the hall towards the front door. "Watch out! He's coming!"

"Do you hear yelling?" Corey asked Brooke as they left the car and made their way around the side of the house to see if there was a window they might peek in through.

"Yeah, I do," Brooke said. "Shit! What's going on in there?"

Each of them had a Molotov cocktail in their hands and Brooke held the lighter in her other, ready to get one going at a moment's notice.

They both cried out as the front door slammed open and heavy footsteps trod the boards of the porch. The gaunt figure of Anthony Stevens rounded the corner and charged them.

"Oh, fuck!" Brooke yelled. She tried to light the wet rag in the neck of her Molotov but her shaking hands wouldn't cooperate.

Corey hurled his unlit Molotov at Anthony and it bounced off his forehead with a loud 'clunk' but didn't break. It landed in the weeds by the side of the house which cushioned its fall.

Brooke had finally succeeded in lighting her own and she drew back her arm to hurl it.

"Let him have it, Brooke!" Corey yelled.

She hurled it and it sailed over Anthony's shoulder, barely singing his hair to land on the ground behind him with a smash and an expanding pool of blue flame.

"Fuck!" said Corey and they both turned and ran, circling the house to the overgrown yard at its rear.

An old barn leant precariously to one side, its boards warped and loose. A door hung slack on rusted hinges, and they made for it, not to hide, but to see if there was anything inside that they might use to dispatch Anthony Stevens in some other manner. Besides, anything was better than pelting through the moonlit woods with him on their trail.

As soon as they were inside, Brooke turned and tried to heave the barn door shut. Corey helped her and they just managed to get it closed before Anthony's bulk slammed against it, making the old hinges rattle.

Brooke slid the bolt across, and they both took a step back as the pounding of his fists reverberated through the barn. He quickly ceased his assault and began looking for another way in. They saw him pass by the grimy and cracked window and they rushed to the other end of the barn to make sure the back door was secure. It was, and they started looking around for something to arm themselves with.

Like the house, the barn had been stripped of pretty much everything. Empty shelves were marked by grimy rings where jars had once stood, and the outline of tools and farming equipment showed on the walls. Among the detritus of teenage partying like broken beer bottles and faded porno mags, there was a rusty length of chain in the corner and a pitchfork that was in such poor repair, nobody had bothered claiming it. As Anthony began hammering on the rear door, Corey seized the pitchfork and pointed at the rusty chain.

"You think we could chain him up somehow and then go back to the car for more Molotovs?" he asked Brooke.

"I don't exactly wanna get close enough to chain him up!" said Brooke.

"You got any better ideas?"

"OK, so, what's the plan? Run out and try and snare him?"

"Uh, I don't think we have to go to him ..." said Corey, looking at the window. "He's coming to us!"

Hands smashed through the windowpane and the head and torso of the killer burst through the glass and splintered frame, reaching, clawing for them. Brooke screamed and they backed up against the far wall, watching in horror as Anthony hauled himself through the small aperture, the rends in his flesh from the razor-sharp shards of glass unbleeding and unnoticed.

Like an eel, he slithered through the window and into the barn. Glass fell from his body as he rose, glaring at them with those black pits in his skull.

"Corey!" Brooke wailed. "What do we do?"

"Wait until he's between us and the supporting beam over there," Corey said, jabbing with his pitchfork at a large, square cut timber that supported the hayloft.

They backed away as Anthony advanced, moving steadily towards the front end of the barn.

"Ready with that chain, Brooke!" said Corey as he lowered the prongs of his pitchfork and aimed them at Anthony's chest. "Now!"

Corey broke into a run and Anthony lurched forward to meet him. The prongs of the pitchfork slid into his chest and pushed him backwards. Corey screamed and kept pushing, the might of a terrified ten-year-old overcoming the strength of the dead.

Anthony grunted as his back slammed against the supporting timber and the pitchfork punched deeper into his chest, its prongs embedding in the wood behind him, pinning him to the timber.

"Now, Brooke!" Corey yelled, not daring to let go of the pitchfork in case the pinned man detached himself from the pillar.

Brooke swung the end of the chain with all her might. It struck Anthony across the neck and wound around both him and the pillar.

"Run around him!" Corey yelled.

Brooke did so, winding the chain around and around Anthony who jerked and wriggled, gripping the prongs that penetrated his chest, trying to wrench the implement loose.

"We did it!" Corey cried, letting go of the pitchfork at last. "Come on! Before he wriggles free!"

They opened the barn door and ran out into the yard.

The blackness beneath the house was impenetrable but Lauren knew she had to make her way through it if she was going to escape. The cellar door at the top of the stairs was too solid; there was no getting out that way. If she wanted to save Corey and Brooke, then she had to find another way out.

She hoped the Stevens house was one of those old farmhouses with a slanted trap door leading to the cellar. She didn't remember seeing one from the outside, but it was a good bet there was one somewhere back there in that inky blackness.

She reached the bottom of the stairs and moved forward, with arms outstretched like a blind person, feeling her way about and trying not to think of what else might be down there. Spiders were the least of her concern, rats too. There could be piles of sharp junk or deep pits that might swallow her whole if she put a foot wrong.

The floor was hard-packed earth and she felt about with her toes before each step, trying to ignore the sticky cobwebs that clung to her face and lips. She bumped into a row of shelves and felt her way along them, her fingers trailing in the dust and rat droppings.

When she reached the far wall, she worked her way along the rough stone and smiled when she felt a cool trickle of night air on her face from somewhere above her. In fact, if she squinted, she could make out a thin sliver of moonlight and knew that there had to be a door somewhere back there.

Then, her feet bumped against some stone steps. She smiled, despite the desperate situation. She had found the way out!

Feeling her way up the steps on her hands and knees, her head bumped against the inclined wood of the trapdoor. Now, if only there was some sort of latch ...

She found it. Her fingers felt the outline of a simple bolt and, once she had it visualized in her head, she was able to slide it back and push the door open. Moonlight dazzled her and she gulped down lungfuls of fresh air as she stumbled up the steps.

Then she heard running feet approaching her from the darkness of the yard.

CHAPTER 19

"Lauren!" Brooke screamed as she and Corey came running towards her. "You're OK?"

"Yeah," said Lauren as she pulled cobwebs out of her hair. "I'm fine, but why did you guys follow me?"

"Because you needed our help, dummy!" Corey said. "We've got old Stevens tied up in the barn. We're going back to the car for some Molotovs so we can blow his ass to the moon!"

"He's in the barn?" Lauren asked, uncertainly. She had come to learn that nothing was a sure thing regarding her father.

"Chained up with a pitchfork jammed in his chest," said Brooke. "But we don't know for how long. Come on, hurry!"

They rounded the house to the front drive where the two vehicles were parked. Opening the trunk of Mrs. Lutz's Audi, Brooke handed Molotovs to Corey and Lauren, taking the final one herself.

"Three boom bottles," said Corey. "That outta be enough to roast that old bastard!"

"Let's just get this done so we can go home," said Brooke. "I don't know how we're going to explain any of this."

They headed back around the side of the house and made their way across the yard towards the barn.

"OK," said Corey. "This a safe enough distance you think? Shall I throw first or shall we all do it together?"

"Wait," said Lauren. "I want to see him. I want to be completely sure he's in there before we torch the barn."

"Lauren, let's just do it!" Brooke pleaded. "Don't take chances now!"

"My father has a nasty habit of surviving," Lauren said. "And I mean before you guys turned him into a zombie. I need to see him with my own eyes."

They headed into the barn with nervous caution. It took a while for their eyes to grow accustomed to the gloom but, when they did, Brooke let out a small whimper of terror.

The supporting timber was bare. The length of rusty chain cast to one side. And the pitchfork was missing.

"He escaped!" said Brooke. "Oh, Jesus, he escaped!"

"Calm down," Lauren told her. "He'll be around here somewhere. We just need to find him and then unleash what we have on him."

They backed out of the barn and looked around the shadow-haunted yard. The long grass wavered in the wind. Of their prey, there was no sign.

"Back in the house, you figure?" asked Corey.

"God, I hope not!" said Brooke.

"We need to check," said Lauren. "We need to make sure we finish this."

They headed towards the rear of the house with its tattered screen door that led into the kitchen. Before they reached it, Lauren heard the thud of boots on grass and turned just in time to see her father rushing towards them from the nearby trees with a pitchfork held low and pointed at Corey.

"Watch out!" she yelled as she barreled into Corey, knocking him flat. As she fell on top of him, the tip of the pitchfork grazed her side, cutting her flesh down to the ribs. She gasped in pain and felt the hot wetness of blood immediately soak through her sweater. The Molotov fell from her grip and landed somewhere in the long grass. She could hear Brooke screaming and knew she had to get them away from him; get Brooke and

Corey to a safe enough distance so they might be able to hit him with their Molotovs now that hers was lost.

Anthony Stevens had stumbled headlong against the wall of his own house, his pitchfork now reddened with his daughter's blood. Before he could get to his feet, Lauren was dragging Corey away with one hand and clutching her bleeding side with the other, Brooke supporting her other side.

"Burn him!" she yelled. "Light him up!"

Brooke and Corey struggled to light their bottles. Corey got his lit and passed the lighter to Brooke. He drew back his arm and threw his Molotov. Anthony ducked and it smashed against the wall of the house, a brilliant blue pool of fire spreading across the planks and curling the paintwork.

"Shit!" Corey exclaimed.

It was down to Brooke now. She was their only chance. She lobbed her blazing Molotov and Anthony, in a blinding display of articulation, wheeled the handle of his pitchfork around to smash it before it hit him.

Some of its contents did land on him however, and liquid fire splashed his arm, working its way up to his shoulder and singing his straggly hair. He moaned and wailed as he dropped the pitchfork and started to thrash at his burning arm, not feeling the pain but sensing that if the fire spread, it could destroy him.

The three of them stood and stared as he whacked and beat at his own arm, each of them willing the fire to win and consume him utterly. But their luck was on a filthy streak that night and he succeeded in extinguishing the fire with his hand, not caring about burning that one too, clamping it down on the flames which had turned from blue to yellow as they started to eat his clothes and flesh.

"Uh, what now?" Corey asked as Anthony, smoke rising from his fire-ravaged arm, bent down to pick up his pitchfork.

"Back to the car," said Lauren. "Run!"

They turned and sped around the side of the house. It was hopeless. They were trying to fight the supernatural with everyday household items. What had they been thinking?

The Lipstadt's station wagon was closest, and they piled into it just as Anthony lumbered around the corner of the house, pitchfork raised in the triumph of the chase. Lauren slid the key into the ignition and the old bucket spluttered into life. She placed her foot on the gas pedal and hesitated.

"What are you waiting for?" Brooke yelled from the passenger seat. "Get us out of here!"

"Lauren, he's coming right at us!" Corey cried over her shoulder.

"No," Lauren said with finality. She had come here to finish this and that was what she was going to do, no matter what it took.

She popped the car into first and pressed down on the gas. The wheels spun erratically, kicking up sprays of dirt as the vehicle gained traction. It swerved from side to side as Lauren fought the uneven terrain, eventually straightening out and heading directly towards Anthony.

Brooke screamed and covered her eyes. Corey sank down in the back seat. Lauren yelled defiance at her father. She yelled out all the pent-up misery and anger of the past five years. She yelled for her childhood which had been a lie and she yelled for all the people who had been killed because a town had let its prejudice get the better of it.

And then, the front of the car slammed into her father, bending him nearly double as his head and torso slapped down on the hood while his feet and legs were sucked under the bumper.

Lauren didn't take her foot off the gas for a second and they continued around the side of the house, ploughing Anthony Stevens before them.

He writhed on the hood, which was slick with a dark, greenish liquid that seeped out of his shattered face and rose up from his crushed abdomen in a vomit of slime. As they rumbled into the back yard, the long grass tugged at the wheels and Lauren knew she would not be able to continue forever, though part of her wanted to. She slammed on the brakes and Anthony shot off the front of the vehicle and landed somewhere in the undergrowth.

Lauren's chest heaved with exertion, and only then did she realize that she had been screaming the whole time. Brooke peeped through her fingers at her, and she could see Corey's pale face in the rearview mirror.

"I told you that we would finish it tonight," Lauren said, turning to half-smile at her traumatized passengers.

"He's up!" Brooke said, pointing through the windshield at the figure of Anthony rising from the weeds on shattered bones, his body crooked and broken. His pitchfork was long gone but he stood there in the headlights like a mangled and rat-eaten scarecrow, his ruined face gazing blindly into the light like a deer about to become roadkill.

"Not this time," said Lauren through gritted teeth and she slammed her foot down on the gas once more.

The car rocketed forward. If Anthony knew what was coming towards him, then he showed no inkling of caring. Once more, the car slammed into him, scooping him up like a ragdoll but this time, Lauren spun the wheel and aimed the car towards the house.

"Seatbelts!" she yelled to her passengers.

Brooke and Corey fumbled to strap themselves in as the rear of the Stevens house rapidly approached; a background to the flailing body of Anthony Stevens being carried towards it.

Lauren's forehead struck the steering wheel as the car ploughed into the back of the house, smashing through its rotten boards and crashing into what had been the dining room. Sharp pain erupted through her sinuses as her head bounced back and hit the cushioned headrest. She saw stars and heard only ringing.

Then, a voice.

"Lauren? Lauren?"

It was Brooke, frantically shaking her by the shoulder.

"I'm ... OK," said Lauren, clutching her throbbing forehead. She felt warm blood under her fingernails. "I can't see anything."

"That's because we're inside the house," said Corey behind her. "Can you reverse?"

"Wait," said Lauren as she felt around for the shifter. She put the car in reverse and eased down on the gas pedal. The wheels spun and the car started to vibrate. A horrible groaning of twisted metal and sharp, splintered wood raking the paintwork filled the interior of the car. Inch by inch, she slid it out of the hole until finally it was free, idling in the long grass, its smashed radiator steaming.

Lauren switched the engine off and, groggily, the three of them got out of the car.

Anthony Stevens was no longer affixed to its front. He was in the wreckage of the house, lying in the center of the hole like an asteroid in its crater, his body pierced in a dozen paces by sharp splinters of wood. Still, he moved and twitched, a ruined semblance of life, trapped in the jaws of the house that had spawned him.

The car had shoved him deep into the dining room and, behind him, Lauren could see the crumpled dining table he had once made her sit at with the corpse of her mother. The case of Molotovs she had placed on it, overturned with its contents, some of them miraculously unbroken, scattered throughout the debris.

Lauren and Brooke stared at the ruined mess of a man before them while Corey began rooting about in the weeds. He found what he was looking for; the Molotov Lauren had dropped when Anthony had rushed them with the pitchfork.

"You wanna do the honors?" he said to her, holding out the Molotov in one hand and a lighter in the other.

Lauren accepted them and took a step towards the shape that had once been her father. Through his smashed face, he could somehow detect that she was near and what was left of his lips and his splintered teeth tried to form that word once more; "Lllll …. Lllaurennn …"

Lauren lit the rag of the Molotov and the light of it burning seemed to excite the remains of her father for he began to writhe more spasmodically, trying to reach for her with his broken arms, his lips still trying to say her name.

"Lllaurennn!"

"Go to hell, dad," Lauren said, and she threw the Molotov.

She didn't aim for his head or any other part of his body. She aimed for the cluster of Molotovs which had tumbled into the wreckage behind him. They smashed on impact and a fireball bloomed in the center of the crater, consuming air as it expanded, roaring up through the guts of the house. It engulfed Anthony, washing over him, part liquid, part gas, all inferno.

The stood back and watched him burn for a while, his pinioned limbs writhing. There was no screaming, only a guttural moan and the sizzling of body fat as it cooked, giving more fuel to the fire. Soon, the whole side of the house was ablaze and the heat of it forced them back even further. They could no longer see him in any case. The fire completely obscured him and at last, consumed him.

Lauren said nothing as they watched the house burn. Somebody would see the light from the highway and call the fire department. It would be too late by the time they got there to save either the house or its most recent tenant. By the time the blue flashing lights made their way up from the highway, Anthony Stevens would be long gone.

Like dust in the wind.

CHAPTER 20

For weeks, Sheriff Weiss and the rest of his department tried to puzzle it all together. There were far too many moving parts for Weiss's liking. Lauren, Brooke and Corey all gave the same far-fetched story and Sheriff Weiss had his suspicions that it had been somewhat rehearsed. Anthony Stevens *had* returned. They had all seen him. Brooke and her delinquent friends had decided to defy the curfew and break into the school for a late-night party. Stevens, who had been prowling in the area, had burst in on them and killed Gary, Todd and Toby in quick succession.

Stevens had then kidnapped little Corey Lutz and driven the Lipstadt's station wagon to his old house in the woods. Brooke and Lauren had followed in Mrs. Lutz's car. They had managed to get Corey back and lit the old Stevens house up like a bonfire with Stevens inside it. Dental records proved that he had been incinerated in the inferno and that was the only thing that satisfied Sheriff Weiss. Stevens was dead at last, but the rest of it stunk.

Oh, it was all thought through well enough. Why wouldn't Stevens, a convicted child molester, take Corey back to his house? In fact, the whole escapade made Lauren and Brooke look like the heroes of the piece, despite their irrational disregard for the law and refusal to involve the police. They had saved a kid from a convicted child molester and mass murderer before sending the bastard to his grave.

The only thing was, Sheriff Weiss had known since 1968 that Anthony Stevens hadn't been a child molester.

He'd only been a rookie cop at the time. Old Ron Dorf had been sheriff back then, God rest his soul. That old hard-ass had been born to come down hard on teenage punks and it hadn't taken much to convince him that a weird kid like Anthony Stevens was a kiddie-fiddler. Sheriff Dorf was great pals with Jeff Mackenzie's father too and the whole story about Stevens being seen in the vicinity of the assault on those two girls had been swallowed without question. Then there was the testimony of the two girls which, even a young cop like Weiss knew was bogus. Those two kids had given the story they'd been coached to give. They'd pointed the finger at Stevens and probably believed it too. Young minds are easily bent from what he'd seen in his twenty years as a cop. But what could he have done back then, fresh on the department? All he knew was that whoever had molested those two girls hadn't been Antony Stevens.

So, the story didn't add up quite as neatly as the three survivors seemed to think it would and that wasn't all. Weiss had grilled them at length and put all the obvious questions to them. Why had Lauren – who was known to be a target for bullying at the hands of the other four – have driven out to the school to party with them when she was supposed to be babysitting Corey Lutz? With a reputation as a responsible girl, not to mention an ostracized social pariah, it was completely out of character for her. But she had shrugged and told him that they had invited her to a party and, desperate to fit in, she had foolishly gone along, bringing young Corey with her. Maybe there was some truth in that as kids at the school had informed him that whatever friction had existed between Lauren and Brooke McKenna was a thing of the past and the two girls even seemed to be friends now.

They were covering something up, Weiss was sure of it, but what it was, he simply couldn't fathom. Much of what had happened that night would undoubtedly remain a mystery for all time. If the three survivors wouldn't talk, then only the dead knew the truth.

Weeks after the whole thing had settled down and Crimson Bay had been plunged into another period of grief matching the one five years ago, Lauren and Brooke drove out to the bridge after school where the highway crossed the river. There was certainly a lot of talk about how the two of them seemed to be getting on now; the bully and the bullied, hanging out after school and driving off together with the orange leaves of fall spiraling in the wake of the Lipstadt's newly repaired station wagon, but then, there were far too many questions about that night altogether. Whatever had happened, it had drawn the two of them close together and formed a bond that nobody, not even Valerie Michaels and Jackie Hunter could fathom.

Lauren parked on the verge and they both got out. They walked in silence, out onto the bridge and stood above the foaming water and watched it for a while in silence. Then, with slow deliberation, Lauren pulled the book of spells from her jacket pocket and they both looked at it.

"I don't know why you've waited this long to get rid of it," said Brooke.

"Me neither," Lauren replied. "I guess I just wanted to hold on to the final piece of the puzzle. Once it's gone, then there is nothing left. It's like the last piece of my father."

"And you're ready to let it ... *him* go?" Brooke asked uncertainly.

"Oh, yeah."

Of all the hard questions that had been asked of the two girls over the past few weeks, nobody had asked about the book because, besides Corey, nobody alive knew of it. Nobody knew that it was the key to the whole thing. The town had accepted their story, hastily cobbled together and full of holes though it was. Even Sheriff Weiss, who Lauren was sure smelled a rat, gave in and stopped asking them questions.

The funerals had gone on for weeks. First was Todd's, his parents having cut their vacation short to come home and bury their youngest son. Then came Gary's with his broken father supported by Suzanne, the girlfriend who had translated the book of spells which had brought such misery and fresh horror to Crimson Bay. Suzanne was oblivious to her part in all this and that was the way they had to keep it. It all felt like acting in a play, standing there and pretending that half of what had happened hadn't.

Toby's funeral had been the worst, at least as far as Lauren and Brooke were concerned. Many people in Crimson Bay had lost more than one loved one during the past five years, but Mrs. Johnson, having first lost her husband and then her boyfriend to Anthony Steven's knife, then had to suffer losing her son as well. She had stood there, almost zombie-like with grief as they had lowered him into the ground, and she held on to Toby's little sister with both hands, as if she might be snatched away from her too at any moment. And the worst of it was that Lauren and Brooke had had to stand there and pretend that her dead son hadn't been a deranged creep who had tried to kill them and was responsible for a few more deaths besides. Lauren, who had always loved theatre, almost found *that* part too hard to play. She had wanted to scream, to cry to tell the truth to all of them. But she couldn't. They had agreed.

The script was written, and she had to say the lines with as much conviction as she could muster.

As they stood there on the bridge, a sharp pain in Lauren's side reminded her of the wound her father had given her. They'd only taken the stitches out a couple of days ago, and the scar was purple and vivid. It would fade to white after a while, she knew, but it would be there always; the last scar her father had given her. All things healed a little, given time, but not everything faded away completely.

"Lauren?" Brooke asked.

"Hmm?" she replied, realizing that she was still holding the book and had been staring at it in silence. "Oh. Yeah. Time to get rid of this damned thing."

It slipped from her fingers, almost without her realizing that she had let go. They watched it spiral and float down to the rushing water and then it was gone, swept away on the foaming current.

They should have burned it along with Anthony Stevens in the inferno of his house, but it had slipped Lauren's mind at the time. The river would do just as well. The ink would run, and the pages would disintegrate just as the dead should do. But most importantly of all, it would be carried out of Crimson Bay, the last vestiges of evil swept away.

"It's over," said Brooke.

"Yeah," Lauren replied.

They headed back to the car and, turning it around, drove back towards Crimson Bay, passing through the shadows and orange leaves that blew down from the slopes of Mount Lenzi.

Printed in Dunstable, United Kingdom